True Vermilion

In This Series

That First Heady Burn

True Vermilion

The Dark Shill

A Stack of Sawbucks

The Hillside Roble

The Peroxide Pomp

The Incidental Twin

Brawl in Bardo

The Window-Shade Job

The Convenient Patsy

The Artisanal Grifter

Shrink in the Shadows

Project Chartreuse

From a Desert Playa

The Tired Canary

A Desperate Frame-up

Trail of the Blue Agave

The Saucer-Heads

DAGMARMIURA.COM

True Vermilion

True Vermilion

George Bixley

DAGMAR MIURA

LOS ANGELES

Published by Dagmar Miura
Los Angeles
www.dagmarmiura.com

True Vermilion

This is a work of fiction. Names, characters, businesses, places, events, and incidents are either the products of the author's imagination or used in a fictitious manner. Any resemblance to actual persons, living or dead, or actual events is purely coincidental.

First published 2018

ISBN: 978-1-942267-53-9

ONE

S later popped the lever on his chair and leaned back, swinging his boots up onto his desk. It wasn't bad, this office, and if he got some work, he might even be able to pay his half of the rent. If he could resist punching his business partner's lights out, there was a good chance they could make a go of it here. The money part could happen today—his primary employer, Della, was on her way over. She worked for an insurance company, having him look into claims around Los Angeles when the bean counters got nervous about making a payout. With any luck she'd need him for a major job, the kind the desk jockeys were willing to pay a premium on to avoid getting their own hands dirty.

When Della walked in, her brow was furrowed

with concern, but her expression softened when she found Slater. He never saw that in her—she was usually relaxed, confident—but they'd only ever met on her turf, in her office. Today she wore chunky heels and a low-cut print dress with a tight waist, accentuating the curvy figure that belied her age, maybe late fifties. Her hair was sprayed into place, swept behind her ears. Slater swung his feet off the desk and stood up.

"You found it."

"Your front door was open," Della said, "but there's no name on it."

"We'll get to that. We just got the furniture in here over the weekend."

"I almost didn't come up. I thought I had the wrong address—it looks like an office building, but inside, it's not." She hefted her bag, the size of a briefcase but made of fabric with loop handles, onto his desk.

"There are offices in it," Slater said, but she was right, it was mostly sewing factories, open floor space with cutting tables, sewing machines, long rolls of fabric stacked on shelves up to the ceiling. Even here, inside the office, Slater could hear the hum of sewing machines cycling on and off. The lobby and stairwells were grungy and gritty like a factory, with peeling paint and ancient linoleum blackened by innumerable feet over the decades, but his little offices behind the elevators had a fresh coat of paint, plus the new furniture he and Max had rented.

"Who are all those people hanging around the front door?" Della asked.

"Day laborers," Slater said. "They take jobs cutting or sewing or carting stuff around. They're mostly gone by three."

"It's too bad you don't have a window in here."

"I've never had an office before, so I'm loving it." He scanned her face. "If it's too much, I can come to your office next time."

She grinned. "You know I'm not one to clutch at my pearls."

"Let me show you around. This is my office, obviously." He waved at the space and walked past her, catching a whiff of her perfume. He didn't know the name of it, but it was distinctive, and he associated it only with her. He stepped into the tiny front office, bare except for a small desk with a wan-looking *Pothos* on it. "This is the reception area."

"Do you have a receptionist?" Della asked, standing behind him.

"Someday, maybe. This is Max's office." He knocked on the door adjacent to his with a knuckle, then pushed it open.

Max was sitting behind his desk, looking at his cell phone, and rose when they came in. In his forties, he had a sloppy haircut and wore a rumpled brown suit, his shirt open at the collar. He looked exactly like what he was: the heavy, his sidearm bulging under his jacket.

"I'm glad one of you has a window," Della said.

Max grinned at her. "If I crane my neck the right way, I can almost see the sky. You must be Della. Slater didn't tell me you were so beautiful."

Della chuckled, pointing her thumb toward Slater. "He's totally oblivious to anything without a dick."

Max guffawed, throwing his head back.

Almost as an afterthought, Della said, "Thanks for the compliment. That's a risky opening, by the way, commenting on my appearance."

"I figured you could probably handle it," Max said, holding her gaze.

Della put a hand on her hip. "Aren't you the cocky bastard."

"Would you two knock it off with the hetero-speak?" Slater demanded. "It's like watching an Italian movie without the subtitles."

"Such a chauvinist," Della said to him, and to Max, as if sharing a confidence, "Are you happy with your new office?"

"I know it's a little rough, but it's nice to have a place to come to do business," Max said. "I've never spent time in this neighborhood, but I like it—the parking is cheap, plus Slater fits right in with most of the people working in the building."

Slater was dark, as his father was Latin American, and probably more indigenous than Spanish, and it was true that he looked like everyone who worked in production here, looked like half the people in the city. But still, being typecast made him want to punch the smirk off Max's ugly mug. He shot him a murderous look.

"What?" Max demanded. "You told me yourself someone out front offered you a delivery job."

Slater sighed. "That did happen." He swallowed his ire, not wanting to go off on him in front of Della, and have her think he was more of a hothead than she already did. Besides, he had to work with Max. More than anyone else, he had to figure out how to tolerate him.

"Are you each working on your own cases," Della asked, looking at Max, "or are you collaborating?"

"Both, hopefully," Max said, glancing at his phone. "I've actually got a job this afternoon. I should go."

"Babysitting?" Slater asked.

"Right," Max said, slipping his phone into his jacket pocket.

"You're not actually doing child care," Della said, frowning.

"'Babysitting' means working as a bodyguard for rich people who think anywhere east of La Brea is the Third World," Max said. "Today we're going shopping on Melrose, apparently."

Della scoffed. "Watch out for IEDs."

Slater followed Max out of his office, heading into his own as Max left. Della sat in front of his desk in the lone extra chair.

"So why did you set up shop with Max?" she asked. "He doesn't seem like your type."

"That's why he's the perfect business partner. He has a PI license, so he can do things that I can't. He's not too smart, but he's not afraid of hard work. Plus I trust him. I met him on that Gislitech job, and he did the right thing—he helped me end it."

"Trust is huge," she said, nodding. "Way more important than all that other stuff."

Slater scooted his chair closer to the desk. "So what have you got for me?"

Della reached into her bag and pulled out a sheaf of paper, bound at one corner by a binder clip, and dropped it on the desktop with a slap. "Stolen property. It's a huge claim, a hundred and seventy-five grand, and for a single piece—a necklace. It's making the actuaries nervous."

"This, I've got to see," Slater said, and picked up the sheaf, leafing through until he found a page with a laser-printed image. Like so many jewelry photos taken for insurance, the necklace was arrayed on a blue background, with a quarter placed at one edge to show the scale. The piece sparkled in the camera's flash, five long strands studded with innumerable white stones—those had to be diamonds—and a cluster of larger red stones in the middle, ringed with even more diamonds. Flipping the page, the next image was a close-up of the central stones, and then another of the clasp, the quarter dutifully in place but so large that he could see the waves in George Washington's hair.

"That's a lot of rocks," Slater said, flipping back to the first picture.

"Tell me about it. Can you imagine wearing that? They could see you from space."

"The cops are looking into it?"

"They say they are," she said, gesturing helplessly, "but they haven't interviewed anyone, at least not to my knowledge, except what the patrol cops did the night it was reported."

"Was it on someone's neck?"

"It wasn't a mugging. The claimant took it off and left it on a table for a short time, and then it was gone. She was in an office with no security, so it could have been anyone, it seems, even someone off the street."

"That explains the cops' disinterest," Slater said. "What do you want me to find out?"

"Look into her, and assess whether she might be lying."

"You think she's still got it? She could never

wear it again, or even try to sell it. It's too unique. You think maybe she's going to separate the diamonds and sell them piecemeal?"

"That's one possibility. With the insurance settlement, she'd get paid for it twice."

"Was anyone else with her?"

"The theft happened at the family business, a clothing company, but it was after hours. There were four or five people there, including the claimant's husband, who owns the business. He swears his employees are completely trustworthy."

"That sounds totally suspicious," Slater said.

"It's all in the paperwork." Della nodded to the sheaf and rose from her chair. She cocked her head, looking at the wall behind Slater. "Is that a safe?"

"Sweet, right?" Slater said, rising and stepping aside so that she could admire it. "Max and I went in on it together. The bolts were still in the floor."

Della raised an eyebrow. "Bolts?"

"A safe has to be bolted down. Otherwise any knucklehead could walk off with it. This building is almost a hundred years old, and in those days, every office had a safe. They put the bolts in when they poured the concrete."

"What do you keep in there?"

"Don't ask."

Della watched him for a moment. "You live in a very different world."

"That's what you pay me for."

"Always good to see you," she said, looping the handles of her bag over her arm and moving toward the door. "Congrats on the new office. You know, there's some good food around here. You should let me take you out."

Slater scoffed. "You do this every time I see you, Della. You know I only date guys. Didn't you tell me you had a beau these days?"

She grinned. "I do. Macking on you is just perfunctory."

"Perfunctory, like saying good-bye," Slater said pointedly.

Della waved as she left.

Sitting down again, feet on the desk, Slater read through the paperwork. The claimant, Lillian Kawada, wrote that she'd been at her husband's office, implying that she didn't work there with him, even though Della had characterized it as the family business. She had set the necklace on a table, walked away to change clothes, and three minutes later, returned to find it gone. In the box for the date and time she'd written 6:40 p.m. That meant it had been well after dark, with winter's limited hours of daylight. The location was listed as Kawada Couture, and judging by the address it was just a few blocks from here, a little farther from downtown in the same neighborhood, the Fashion District, a dense cluster of clothing manufacturers and suppliers. It was still business hours—Slater could drop in at the scene of the crime.

Della hired him to take care of things a big company couldn't get away with, despite their vast resources, and one of the tools he had that fell outside their capabilities was an ex-boyfriend named Conrad. The guy was a total idiot, but he worked as a cop, right in Slater's neighborhood, and Slater was able to coerce him from time to time into providing information on the lowlifes he came across in his cases.

Slater slept with lots of guys, and never let himself get sticky with any of them, but he'd fallen for this one, and opened up, made himself vulnerable. After a disastrous attempt at a relationship, Conrad had summarily dumped him, trampling him like a piece of trash.

Before that had happened, though, when things were still good, Slater had managed to put a hidden tracking app on Conrad's phone. It was his own stupid fault, Slater reasoned, for letting him see the code he used to unlock it. You'd think a cop would be a little more security-conscious. It wasn't really invasive, because it was useful but not very interesting to see Conrad's location; he was usually at his stupid job or his stupid house, undoubtedly playing his stupid video games.

Pulling up the tracking app on his phone, he

found Conrad on the 101, moving through the Cahuenga Pass at freeway speed. Hopefully he was headed to his station, the lazy moron. Most self-respecting desk jockeys were at work by now. Conrad sometimes worked patrol, but it was better for Slater when he was at the station.

After he stuffed Della's paperwork into his canvas satchel and slung it over his shoulder, he headed out. Della was right—they needed to put their names on the office, he saw, as he locked up. Otherwise it was just a numbered door. Still, he felt the satisfaction of it being his own place.

The elevator had an iron-mesh accordion gate, giving the place an antiquated vibe. At least it slid open by itself when the car arrived. He punched the DOWN button and soon was in the lobby, walking through the dwindling throng of day laborers hanging around the entrance. It was two long blocks to Kawada Couture, which turned out to be in a high-rise full of clothing manufacturers, like his own building but a little bigger, and newer, and cleaner. The entrance was devoid of the colorful array of sticky notes with job offers and phone numbers that decorated his building, and no one was hanging out waiting for work either. Della wouldn't have balked at walking in here.

There was no security desk, and the board with the list of tenants showed only the floor number for Kawada Couture. Scanning the lobby, a lone camera was mounted above the elevator, pointed at the entryway, and there were none in the elevator. No wonder the cops weren't pursuing the theft.

The elevator doors opened in the middle of a manufacturing operation—sewing machines under the windows along two walls, rolls of fabric stacked on end, a small army of canvas dressmaker's torso forms, and cutting tables in the middle. The whole floor was Kawada Couture, it seemed, and it was easy to see how someone could walk in unnoticed—he'd just done it.

Lillian had reported it as an office, but it was really a factory, a big open space with no internal walls. The only signs of white-collar work were a conference table and chairs at one end and three desks facing the big warehouse-style windows in the opposite corner. A guy sat at one of the desks, and eight or ten other people were working at the tables and machines. Facing the elevator was a man carefully cutting fabric with big shears. Glancing up when he saw Slater, he called over to the desk, *"Patrón."* Turning back to Slater, he said something in Spanish, which happened a lot—Slater looked like he should be able to understand.

The guy at the desk turned and rose when he saw Slater, a smile on his face as he walked over. This was the boss, based on his demeanor. Lanky and fluid, he was wearing a sport coat and trendily cut pants, and had a serious haircut with a little gray at the temples. Totally fuckable, Slater decided, before he'd even spoken.

"Steve Kawada," he said.

Slater introduced himself and handed Steve his business card. "I work for Cudahy Mutual Insurance."

"About the necklace," Steve said, examining the card.

"Lillian is your wife?"

"Correct," Steve said, meeting his eye, a smirk on his lips.

He must think she's a real prize, this woman, a trophy. Slater wanted to slap that shit-eating grin off his face, but he suppressed the urge, what with all these witnesses.

"Does she work here?" Slater demanded.

"She came by to try on a dress," Steve said, serious now. "One of the perks of being married to a garment manufacturer is that she gets personally tailored clothes."

"Is Kawada a clothing line?"

Steve shook his head. "We produce small batches for labels and store brands."

"I like your space," Slater said, glancing around. "You get great light."

"Sunshine improves your mood even when

you're inside, wouldn't you say?"

"It's also a very egalitarian setup. If you're the boss, why don't you have your own office?"

"Well, I want to work with my staff, not separate from them."

"A man of the people," Slater said, studying his face. "Where do you have meetings?"

Steve gestured to the far end of the floor, where the conference table sat next to a pair of clothing racks. "That serves as the showroom and meeting room, even though it doesn't have walls."

"And no security cameras."

"We don't need them," Steve said simply.

Not if you're content being a target, Slater thought. "What about the one in the lobby?"

"We asked the management—it wasn't working all that week."

Steve was probably telling the truth about that, Slater decided. The cops would have checked on it themselves, so he'd have no reason to mislead his insurer.

"Can I take some photos?" Slater asked, pulling his phone out of his jeans.

"Be my guest."

"So run through it for me. Where did Lillian leave the necklace?"

"Here." He stepped over to the table where the guy who'd spoken earlier was cutting, and tapped the edge. The worker ignored them, focusing on guiding the shears through the billowy purple fabric.

"She put it down and then went into the changing booth," Steve said, pointing to a dark blue curtain suspended on a rail. Like the privacy curtains in hospitals, the rail ran around three sides and back to the wall.

Slater took a photo of it, with the curtain bunched up at one end, then pulled it around as he stood inside. The cutting table was nearby, but if Lillian had closed the curtain completely, it would definitely be out of view. Stepping out, he took another photo, making a show of holding up his phone and examining the screen. He turned and photographed the table, and then took a surreptitious photo of Steve, pressing the shutter button but not looking at the phone.

"Why do you have a changing booth in your factory?" Slater asked.

"We have private couture clients who come in for fittings. It's very lucrative compared to manufacturing for shops. I can charge them close to retail prices without the middleman taking a cut. People love coming down here to buy their clothes in a factory—it's like an exotic adventure. The downside is that consumers are way more finicky than businesses."

"So Lillian's trying on something you made for her, and the curtain is closed. The necklace is there on the table. Where were you?"

"At my desk, working on the computer."

Slater looked at the trio of desks, separated by low file cabinets. They faced the windows, so anyone working there would have their back to the rest of the room.

"Carolina was here too," Steve said, pronouncing it the Spanish way, "kuh-ro-*lee*-na."

Slater gestured impatiently, waiting for him to continue.

"She's the manager—she basically runs the place." He nodded to the desks. "That's hers, next to mine. She was sitting there the whole time, I'm sure of it."

Slater stepped over to the desks. Steve's was tidy, almost bare, but Carolina's was a mess, with paperwork in piles beside her computer screen. Under her keyboard was a blotter, a calendar, he realized, with notes scrawled in pencil and red and blue ink. Casually shifting the keyboard a few inches, he saw a note in the box with today's date, written in red and double underlined:

8 p.m. floor show

Below it was an address, on Vermont Avenue, probably in East Hollywood, based on the number. Why did that seem familiar?

He turned to Steve. "Can you stand inside the curtain, and I'll sit here?"

"Sure," Steve said, and stepped toward the wall. "You want to recreate the scene of the crime?"

"Something like that," Slater said, and watched as Steve pulled the curtain around him.

Sitting in Carolina's chair, he quickly took a photo of the blotter with tonight's appointment, then scanned the space. Several photos were taped to the wall at the back of her desk, most of them featuring the same woman, who looked to be in her late thirties. This had to be Carolina. As he'd expected, based on her name, she had Latin features, but beyond that she looked nothing like the blue-collar staff. Dark, fashionably styled hair tumbled around her head, and her makeup job was pure glam, consistent in every photo.

She stood with a trio of school-age kids over a birthday cake in one image, and in another had her arm around a guy in a necktie and a sheer dress shirt that revealed his beefy pecs, both of them holding champagne flutes. They didn't have the vibe of married people, and neither was wearing a wedding band. This had to be a boyfriend. The children must be nieces and nephews, he decided, and snapped a photo of the array.

Slater rose and slipped his phone into his jeans when he heard the curtain opening again.

"Are you getting what you need?" Steve asked, frowning.

"Presumably you've searched the factory for the necklace?"

"Top to bottom—every drawer, every machine."

"Who else was here?"

"Just a couple of the sewing machine operators. It was the end of the day, and almost everyone was gone. I didn't see any of them leave their stations."

"Not surprising, considering your back was turned the whole time," Slater said, glancing at the desks.

"I could hear the machines."

"You're sure about that? I'd think you hear them so much that it wouldn't even register. You can say with certainty that you didn't see one of them take it, but you didn't see them not take it either."

Steve's mouth became a hard line. "They're good people, Slater," he said finally, lowering his voice.

Slater met his eye, impressed that he'd remembered his name. That square jaw looked a little less punch-worthy now.

"I know your job is to be suspicious," Steve continued, "but they've been with me for years. Neither one of them would have done this."

"Who were the sewing people working that night?"

"Faith and *hee-may-nah*."

Slater had to think about the name, the Spanish spelling, probably with a *j* or an *x*. Definitely *x*, he decided: Ximena.

"Faith's not in today, but I'll introduce you to Ximena."

Steve walked over to her machine, facing the windows opposite his desk. Ximena was middle-aged, her dark hair pulled back and bound tightly behind her head. She turned in her chair when Steve called her name but didn't rise.

"Ximena, this is Slater. He works for the company that insures Lillian's jewelry."

Slater met her eye and extended his hand. She looked at him for a second, baffled, but shook it anyway. When she was distracted by the handshake, with his phone in his left hand, Slater deftly snapped a photo of her; neither she nor Steve noticed what he was doing.

"I already told everything to the police woman," Ximena said, her tone guarded.

Assessing her, nothing about her was fearful, Slater decided.

"Can you tell me about that night?" he asked, slipping his phone into the pocket of his jeans.

Ximena sighed. "I was working, right here, and suddenly Ms. Lillian is screaming. 'My necklace,'" she mimicked, waving her hands for effect.

"You didn't see anyone come or go?"

"I was trying to finish a piece before I went home. I wasn't looking around. It turned into a late evening, though, with all the screaming and the police."

"I'm sorry that happened," Steve said, his brow furrowed in concern.

Ximena grinned at him and waved dismissively.

"Do you remember anyone hanging around earlier in the day?" Slater asked, his gaze intent. "Anyone who doesn't work here? Maybe someone's boyfriend dropped in?"

Ximena shrugged. "Nothing like that."

"Who do you think took it?"

"I have no idea. I'm sorry I can't help."

Slater nodded and stepped away. "I need to talk to Carolina," he said to Steve, and looked around the factory at the workers, none of whom looked anything like the flashy woman in the photos taped beside her computer. "She's not around?"

"She'll be back tomorrow." Steve went over to his desk and came back with a business card. "You can call her on the office number, and my cell is on there too."

Slater eyed him. The guy wasn't flirting, he decided, and dropped the card into his satchel.

"How well do you know her?" he asked.

"She's worked with me for years," Steve said. "She had nothing to do with this, I'm sure of that.

I'd trust her with my life."

"So who do you think did it?"

Steve shrugged. "No clue."

"How can I talk to Lillian?"

"Drop by the house," Steve said. "We live in Hancock Park."

"I'll do that," Slater said, and turned to go.

"That's all you need?" Steve called after him.

Slater turned back and pointed a finger at him. "If I want more from you, you'll hear about it," he said sharply.

"I'll look forward to it," Steve said, grinning at him.

Standing there assessing him, it took Slater a moment to realize that smile wasn't a challenge. He turned and went to the elevator. Clueless, the guy was, he thought as he rode down—chirpy and oblivious, when most people would have been intimidated. Like a cork that wouldn't sink, it didn't matter how much you glared at him, he was still breezy, upbeat. Why was he so pleasant, so cooperative, so trusting of his employees? Maybe he was just a nice guy, but maybe there was more to it. What was he hiding? Just thinking about that grin made him want to gut-punch the guy, knock him to the ground, just to see if he'd get angry and fight back. Everyone had it in them, even if some buried it more deeply than others.

Walking back to his building, he checked

Conrad's location on his phone. The moron was at his station, finally. Instead of going up to his office, Slater crossed the street to the surface lot where he and Max parked and climbed into his black Thunderbird. It was a '78, and in good shape, so it got more attention than he wanted—he always had to park out of view of where he was going. But he loved it, with its cherry engine and interior, loved the way it handled, loved the horsepower.

Rampart Station wasn't far, just across the freeway on the other side of downtown, but in the afternoon traffic it took him almost half an hour. As he pulled into a street space out front, Slater admired the magnolia trees, three of them along this block, their blossoms huge and white. There was no sign of leafing yet, which made them even more dramatic. Pulling out his phone, he called Conrad's cell.

"Hey, flatfoot," Conrad answered.

"I'm right by your office. Can you come out to talk?"

"Why would you assume I'm at work?"

"Aren't you?"

"Slater, what do you want? You only call me when you need something." Lowering his voice, he added, "I can't be using police resources to help you do your job."

"It's nothing like that. Just put your dick away,

zip up your pants, and come outside."

Conrad sighed. "Give me a minute."

Climbing out of the Thunderbird, Slater waited on the front steps, and soon Conrad appeared, thick and swarthy, barrel-chested in his tight uniform even without the ballistic vest, and just the same height as Slater. Such a beautiful man, despite that dumb cop haircut.

Conrad scowled at the sight of him and waved him over to the accessibility ramp, where there would be less chance of being overheard.

"So how's the new office?" Conrad asked, hands on his hips.

"It's pretty glam—eight thousand square feet, three fireplaces, and from my windows I can see Mount Wilson and the ocean."

"You can't see the ocean from the Fashion District," Conrad said, frowning. "Everything you just said sounds far-fetched."

"You should take the detective exam," Slater said. "It may not be quite that amazing, but I'm happy with it."

"So what are you doing here?"

"I'm glad I caught you at your desk. I'm working an insurance claim. Your people took a report, and I want to know if they're investigating it or sitting on it."

"Why would that matter for what you're doing?"

"I'm not going to do the work if someone else already has."

"So you want me to leak what the detectives have uncovered."

Slater nodded. "That would be great, thank you."

"I'm not going to do that," Conrad said, raising his voice.

"It's just a simple yes-no question to start with. Is anyone working on it? Besides, you know I can make your life a living hell."

"You already did that, and then we broke up, remember?"

Slater scowled. "Fuck you, Conrad. You know what I'm talking about. I have in my possession certain compromising photos."

"Dude, I don't care who sees me naked. My boss would just laugh."

"If you can handle the embarrassment, then it's on you."

"I don't think I even believe you have photos like that. I certainly don't remember you taking them."

Of course he didn't—Slater would never do something like that, not to Conrad—but he needed some leverage over the guy, as ineffectual as Conrad made it sound.

Conrad folded his arms. "I'm not going to leak the case files to you, but I can find out the status of the investigation. Text me the date and the address where we took the report."

"I think that's a wise choice. I doubt that your colleagues would want to see my dick in your mouth."

Conrad grinned and shook his head. "It's almost like you don't get that I'm volunteering to help you. You don't need to work the lame-ass blackmail thing on me. But you keep saying it. It makes me think you'd rather things worked that way."

"You can spin it any way you want, toots," Slater said, holding out his palms. "Whatever helps you sleep at night."

"I'm being nice, Slater. Like a friend. People are nice sometimes."

"You were, sometimes," Slater said wistfully, and turned away.

"My buddies would love to see that photo, by the way," Conrad called after him. "They'd have it printed on my birthday cake."

Ignoring him, Slater climbed into the Thunderbird and twisted the key in the ignition. Why did he have to be nice? He hated that about Conrad, that attitude, that he was so consistent, so even-tempered. Idiot fucking Conrad.

Daylight was fading as he drove the short distance to his apartment in Westlake, a dense and gritty neighborhood that so far had resisted the pounding waves of gentrification, despite being so centrally located. The best thing about the place, two flights above a cell-phone store, was the garage—his own private parking space right off the alley. He pulled in and waited for the heavy shutter to roll down before unlocking the door to the stairwell and trotting up to his dingy one-bedroom, with its generic beige paint job and grimy windows. His thrift-store furniture fit right in, except his bed—the futon, at least, he'd bought new.

Calling it a one-bedroom was generous, as it was mostly a single room with a kitchen at one end and a recliner and a sofa at the other, hiding some of the stained carpeting, with the bedroom off one side. Dropping his satchel beside the sofa, he looked in the fridge, even though he knew there was nothing in it, except a mostly empty bottle of orange juice, a jar of pickles, and some aging mini takeout containers of salsa. Fishing out a pickle, he munched on it as he checked in the cupboards, finding a vegan Pop-Tart. The bourbon was in the next cupboard, he knew—he didn't even have to look, feeling its presence, just sitting there, waiting patiently for him. A good night for Slater involved sex and bourbon, in that order, and tonight he planned to do both.

After he pulled off his boots, he stretched out on the sofa and ate the Pop-Tart, then looked through the photos he'd taken at Kawada Couture. The one of Ximena was a little blurry, but she was still identifiable, and he had clear images of Steve, and of Carolina's photos. What could be so important as to require red ink and a double line under it, he wondered, zooming in on the photo of Carolina's blotter calendar. He looked up the address she'd written and realized why it had seemed familiar—it was Pry-Bar, a place he knew well because it was easy to find guys looking to hook up. He'd never heard of a floor show, but it did host drag performances once in a while.

Even though the bar wasn't off-limits to women, he never saw them there, so it seemed odd that Carolina was going. From her photos Slater knew what she looked like, and seeing her there would give him a chance to observe her outside her job. Plus there was a whole bar full of guys. It was easy to hook up online, but once in a while it was fun to pick up a guy based on his body language, the way he spoke, what he inadvertently revealed about himself face-to-face, which didn't happen on a pocket-size screen. It made the decision easy—tonight, Slater was going out.

TWO

Waking in darkness, he reached for his phone and checked the time. He'd only been asleep for a couple of hours—it was still early.

Running his fingers through his thick black hair in the bathroom mirror, he decided he wasn't so long unshaven that he looked homeless. He pulled on his fake leather jacket, appropriate for a cold February night. He hated that even though it was ethical—not really made out of cowhide— it didn't look ethical, and he hated that he loved the way it looked on him.

Flicking off the room lights, he locked the deadbolt and trotted down to his garage. It was earlier than most people went out, but Carolina had written "eight p.m." There were always guys

around too, if the place was open, and it was easier to negotiate a hookup when less drinking had
been done. He stayed on surface streets driving
up to Hollywood, as the freeway was still bound
to be congested, and found a street space a couple
of blocks from the bar.

The room with the stage was near the entrance,
and the show was already underway, a queen in a
tall bouffant and sequins sparkling in the spot-
light. She was actually singing, and not a pop
tune either, maybe one of her own. Slater pushed
through the crowd, scanning for the familiar brunette. It wasn't hard to spot her, as most of the
spectators were guys. Carolina and three other
women were at a table together at the side of the
room, drinks in hand, despite the cool weather
wearing short cocktail dresses. In such run-of-
the-mill girly garb, there was no mistaking them
for boys in drag.

Standing among the guys listening to the performance, he watched them, girlfriends out for
the evening, drinking and talking and laughing.
The focus seemed to be their camaraderie rather
than the performer on the stage. Carolina seemed
relaxed, confident. She flipped her hair out of her
eyes with regularity, but she wasn't as animated
as her friend in the red dress. At least they knew
where they were—none of the four were macking
on guys.

It wasn't really informative to watch them, he decided after a while, and if he was going to interview Carolina tomorrow, he couldn't approach her now.

Pry-Bar was a labyrinth of connected rooms and dark corners, not by design but because a couple of commercial spaces had been cobbled together and left unrenovated. Slater elbowed his way out of the crowded concert space and went farther inside, where it was quieter. There were already guys in small groups, drinking and talking, but not a lot of solo patrons. Why did people go out with their friends? It's like they didn't even want the chance to hook up.

Two lone guys sat on stools at either end of the bar, and he checked out each of them as he came up to the service mat and waited for the bartender. The one at the far end would do in a pinch, although he looked like he might be chatty, and that polo shirt made him look like he thought he was in Cancún. The other one just looked annoying, with one of those faces you'd rather punch than talk to.

The bartender didn't step over but gestured to Slater with his chin. What a freaking punk, sneering at a customer—he's a goddamn barman, not the king of the Venetians. But he wasn't going to let a bottle boy with an attitude slow him down.

"Corona," Slater called to him, and dropped a bill on the counter. The bartender soon set down his bottle, complete with a slice of lime wedged in its mouth, and took the bill, but Slater wandered away, pressing the lime in with his thumb, not waiting for his change.

He went through the place methodically, stopping when he found a fuckable guy who was on his own, leaning against a wall next to a high table. His head was shaved, and he wore lumberjack plaid and tight leather chaps over his jeans, exuding confidence. But Slater saw through it, saw that flash of insecurity when their eyes met.

"Have you got a drink?" Slater asked, standing next to him and speaking loudly over the music from the stage, a couple of rooms away.

Baldy looked surprised. "Yeah," he said, lifting a beer bottle from the table.

Slater tapped it with the neck of his Corona and looked pointedly down at the guy's pants. "Here's to menswear."

"You like the chaps?"

"I like what's in them. I'm not a fan of leather."

"Then it's your lucky day. These are vinyl."

"Right on," Slater said, nodding approvingly.

"So are you Latino?" Baldy said, leaning toward him to be heard.

Slater frowned. "In a way."

"You speak English really well."

Slater's instinct was to punch him in the face. He knew this kind of guy—he was big but soft, easy to coldcock, and he'd go down like a sack of potatoes. From the look on his face, though, he could tell the guy was intentionally being provocative, and doing it to make a connection.

"That's high praise from an entitled frat boy."

Baldy winced. "Ouch."

"I don't even speak Spanish," Slater said, "and I'd bet money that my name is more Anglo than yours."

"What's your name?"

"Slater."

"That's pretty Anglo. Listen, I was just trying to be funny."

"Yeah, well, your white privilege is showing, Alice."

Baldy shifted uncomfortably. "Don't get steamed."

"If I was steamed," Slater said, meeting his gaze, "you'd be flat on the floor with a broken nose right now. What's your name, gringo?"

"It's DJ," he said cautiously.

"That sounds made up."

"And Slater doesn't?" he demanded.

Slater grinned. "Good answer." He eyed DJ's crotch again, cocking his head for emphasis. "So what do I have to do to get you to take those off?"

"I guess just come home with me," DJ said.

Slater took a long pull from his Corona and set the bottle on the table. "Let's go."

DJ's eyebrows shot up, but he drained his beer and stepped away from the wall. Slater headed for the door, dodging the crowd and the noise spilling out of the performance space, stopping once they were out on the quieter sidewalk.

"I live in Westlake," Slater said.

"You can come to my place, but I don't have my car."

Slater gestured up the block. "I've got wheels."

"I'm not far," DJ said, walking abreast. "Just two metro stops."

"You wore those on the metro?" Slater said, glancing at the pleasing lines of his chaps. "You're braver than me."

"It's a big city. Most people don't judge."

"And you're a big guy. If they do, you can just let the fists fly." Slater absently balled up his hands and held them in front of his chin.

DJ laughed, even though Slater wasn't kidding. "So why don't you like leather?"

"I like the look of it, just not what happens to get it off the cow."

"You're vegan? You so don't look like one."

Slater glanced at him sidelong. "What happened to not judging?"

"Don't get me wrong," DJ said, shrugging. "It's fine by me."

"I don't actually need your permission," Slater said, pulling out his keys and stepping around to the driver's door of the Thunderbird. He climbed in and unlocked the passenger's side.

"You know, you're kind of abrasive," DJ said, after he'd pulled the door closed, "but it's turning me on."

"Don't tell me what I am," Slater said irritably, and started the engine.

DJ reached toward his face, and Slater caught himself before he grabbed the guy's wrist, instead letting him touch his cheek and turn his head, leaning in to kiss him. His mouth was warm, soft and hard in the right way, sour from the beer. This is what it was about, why he was here, Slater remembered, feeling his woody tightening in his jeans. It wasn't about the annoyance, but rather this connection.

"Corona with lime," DJ said softly, pulling back.

"Which way?"

"North," he said, and pointed up Vermont.

Cruising the side street where DJ directed him, Slater couldn't find a parking spot, and circled around the block.

"These neighborhoods, man," he muttered, turning onto another street.

"Isn't Westlake even worse?"

"I have a garage."

Eventually he found a street space, waiting while a woman in a long camel coat stepped into her SUV and got it started, brake lights blinking on, freeing up room for the Thunderbird. After Slater deftly backed in, DJ climbed out and led the way, looping his arm around Slater's waist as they walked. It was sweet, Slater thought, glancing at him.

"I'm on the next corner," DJ said, and Slater stepped behind him to let two young guys pass on the sidewalk.

Moments after they'd gone by, Slater heard one of them mutter "faggots." He spun around and ran a few steps to catch up to them. The shorter one, in a stupid wooly hat with a basketball logo embroidered on it, glanced back, his eyes growing wide, and scurried onto the adjacent lawn just as Slater caught his companion by the collar. He was lightweight and easy to manhandle, and younger than Slater had thought at first, once he'd spun him around, pulling him up by the lapels of his stupid baggy jacket.

"It wasn't me," the guy whined, fear in his eyes. In the periphery Slater saw wooly-hat running up the block. Slater gave the guy a good shake, and he grabbed Slater's arms with both of his, trying to wrench himself away. It was a classic move, instinctive even, based on how many people reacted that way, but it was a big mistake.

Slater threw his hands off by spreading his arms, and then punched him hard in the face.

"Stop it," DJ cried. "They're just morons."

The punk stumbled backward a few steps, dazed, and Slater followed, punching him again.

"Why do you make me do this?" Slater demanded.

Holding out both palms, the guy stepped backward, slumping against a parked van. There was a smear of blood under his nose, Slater saw, even though it looked black in the dimness of the streetlights rather than satisfying bright red. But it was enough just to see it, and he could feel balance returning to the world. He grabbed the guy by his lapels and yanked him to the back of the van, then shoved him out into the street, where he tumbled onto his butt. A passing car slowed down, nosed around him, and honked before roaring away. The guy got up, caught sight of Slater, then staggered across the street, not looking back but picking up speed. Slater watched him trot up the block before turning away.

"Why did you do that?" DJ demanded, facing him on the sidewalk.

"It's part of my educational outreach program," Slater said, stuffing his hands in his jacket pockets. "He might think twice before using that word again."

"You could have killed him."

"Dude—I know what I'm doing. Two little rabbit punches weren't going to do much harm. He won't even have a bruise."

"You threw him into the traffic," DJ said emphatically.

"He didn't get run over." Slater sighed. "You seem upset. Does this mean it's the end of our evening?"

DJ studied him for a second. "No," he said quietly, "I think that's still on."

Slater grinned, and stepped toward him, bumping his shoulder with his own as they walked.

"You'll have to wash the blood off your hands first, though."

DJ's apartment was a classic LA one-bedroom, old but clean, bigger and much nicer than Slater's but probably three times as expensive. The front door opened on the living room, where an acoustic guitar sat on a stand in front of a table with a pro-looking audio board on it.

"You're a musician," Slater said.

"For fun, not for work."

Slater pulled off his jacket, and DJ was already unbuttoning his plaid shirt. Slater watched him take it off, admiring his beefy torso.

"So what are you into?" Slater asked, hands on his hips.

"I usually wind up with twinks," DJ said, stepping closer. "They're like stemware—you have to be careful not to break anything. I never hook up with guys like you."

"You want me to rough you up, like the knucklehead on the street?"

"No," he said, and hesitated, looking serious. "I want to do that to you. Only because I don't think I could do much damage."

"Let's see if that's true. Come at me."

DJ folded his arms. "OK, so, what do you mean? What should I do?"

Slater jerked his chin at him, raising his voice. "Just do it, man. Take your best shot."

Surprise flitted across DJ's face, but then Slater saw that he was working up to it. Clenching his jaw and stepping toward Slater, he slapped his cheek, hard enough to turn his head. An open-handed slap was never going to be anyone's best shot, and the delivery was a bit tentative, but Slater could feel his cock swelling.

"Nice," he said. "I felt that."

"Not too much?" DJ said, biting his lower lip.

"I'll let you know if that happens. Come on, man—manhandle me."

DJ grabbed his wrist and twisted his arm behind his back. He didn't know how to do it effectively, and Slater could have broken free in a nanosecond, but he went along with it, let himself be frog-marched into the bedroom. It was kind of fun not to be the one making the decisions.

DJ pushed him onto the bed, roughly turned him over, and climbed on top, straddling his pelvis.

"Do you want me to unbutton your shirt?"

"You tell me, boss," Slater said sharply. "You're in charge."

"Right," DJ said, and ripped it open.

It was surprising how easily it gave way, fabric tearing, buttons popping off. Slater let him unbuckle his belt, and helped him pull off his jeans. DJ stood over him, leering at his naked form.

"You're hard," DJ said. "You're ready for this."

Propped up on his elbows, Slater watched appreciatively as DJ unbuckled his chaps and took off his jeans. Soon he was on top of Slater again, his flesh hot. He pushed Slater onto his side and wrapped his arm around his neck, pulling tight. He could feel DJ's hard cock pressing into his thigh.

Slater tapped his arm. "Time out."

DJ instantly released his grip. "What did I do?" he asked, worried.

"If you apply pressure with your forearm, you'll crush my trachea, see?" He pulled DJ's arm into position horizontally across his neck. "Then I'm never going to breathe again. If you use the inside of your elbow, you can put pressure on the veins on both sides, and cut off the air without breaking anything." Slater manipulated him again, snugly notching his Adam's apple into the crook of DJ's arm. "See how easy that is? A few seconds of moderate pressure and I'm out like a light, no damage done."

"It's scary that you know that."

"Now you know it too." Slater reached around and grabbed his cock. "Are you ready to fuck me?"

DJ was more confident, more experienced with sex than with the rough stuff, and he kissed Slater intently while he worked his fingers into him, eventually shifting position and sliding his cock inside, gasping at the sensation. He wrapped his arm around Slater's neck at one point in an appropriate choke hold, but didn't use much pressure, instead working up a rhythm with his cock until he was pounding him. Slater leaned into it, relishing the intensity, until DJ came. Once he'd pulled out, he conscientiously stroked Slater's cock, their mouths locked. This guy really knew how to kiss, Slater thought, and got lost in it, and soon came too.

After the moment faded, DJ got up and pulled off his condom, stepping out of the room and returning a moment later with a white hand towel, passing it to Slater as he lay down beside him.

"Such a gentleman," Slater said.

DJ chuckled. "Want to sleep over?"

"I can't, but thanks."

Slater spent a while with his arm around DJ's belly, luxuriating in the warmth of his body, and eventually rose to pull on his jeans, and loop his arms into his ripped-up shirt.

"Sorry about that," DJ said, watching him dress.

"Totally worth it," Slater said, pulling on a boot. "You've got the red mist in you."

"What's the red mist?"

"Rage," Slater said simply. "Everyone has it. It's good to air it out once in a while."

———•———

It was such a great feeling, that time right after sex, he thought, walking to his car. Too bad it didn't last very long. Once he'd climbed the stairs from his garage, he threw his jacket on the recliner and grabbed the bourbon, still waiting for him stoically in the kitchen cupboard. Pouring a hefty volume into a tumbler, he pulled open the freezer and dropped in an ice cube. He savored the aroma for a moment before taking a gulp, reveling in the delicious golden burn. With another sharp mouthful, he could already feel his mind starting to slow down, flatten out.

Pulling off his boots and stretching out on the sofa, he set the tumbler on the floor nearby and found an episode of the *Sasquatch Search* podcast on his phone. He'd never gone tramping around the forest looking for the creature's tracks or listening for their eerie calls, and he wasn't even sure what he believed about bigfoot, but listening to other people talk about it, relating the quest, took him far from this gritty city, its horde of mouthy punks, day laborers, stolen jewelry. Soon he was deep in the woods, warmed through by the glow of liquid amber.

THREE

This was his own bed, he knew, as he woke up, and he was alone, but he couldn't remember how that had happened. Had someone been here? No, that had been somewhere else. His head throbbed as he sat up. Walking to the bathroom, he spotted a half-empty bourbon bottle on the kitchen counter. It seemed like a lot of it was missing, but there was no mystery about where it had gone—he could feel its aftereffects pounding in his temples, sapping his strength.

In the kitchen he pulled the orange juice out of the fridge and drank from the bottle, then microwaved a mug of water, shaking powdered coffee into it from the jar and swirling it around with a spoon. Sipping it made him feel a little better, and he leaned on the counter with his hands wrapped around the warm mug.

His phone rang in the bedroom, and when he retrieved it he saw that it was Conrad, the big dummy—Slater hadn't even checked on his whereabouts yet.

"So officially your theft is an active investigation," Conrad began, "but they gave it to someone with a two-foot pile of cases on her desk. Don't look for action on it anytime soon."

"Is it a low priority because there's no evidence?" Slater asked.

"Maybe, but jewelry and art are often solved when the thieves try to sell the stuff. The detective will probably wait for that to happen."

"Good to know."

"You sound groggy. Rough night?"

"Action-packed, you might say."

"The liquid version?"

"Fuck you, Conrad."

"Have you eaten anything today?" he asked, ignoring Slater's ire.

"I had some fruit. What's it to you, anyway? You're not my mother."

"She told me to ask you."

Slater scoffed. "That's all I need—you and Doris conspiring to make me miserable."

"Nobody's conspiring. We do a spin class together."

"That doesn't sound like either one of you," he

said, grinning at the absurdity of it. "I have to go. Put your dick away and get back to work."

"Back at you," Conrad said.

After he'd splashed some water on his face and thought hard about shaving, eventually rejecting the idea, he pulled on the same jeans he'd worn yesterday, along with a clean shirt—a decent-looking dark one with a collar, as he was going to meet clients. His satchel was on the floor by the sofa where he'd left it, and he riffled through Della's paperwork on the case to find Lillian Kawada's address, punching it into his phone.

Slinging the bag over his shoulder, he trotted down to the garage, grinning again at the idea of Conrad and Doris on stationary bicycles. It had to be fiction. There was the possibility, though, that they were comparing notes. That would be a nightmare. They can't be, he decided. He was being paranoid.

It was just a few minutes' drive to tony Hancock Park and its stately old-money homes, nothing like the newer gated compounds of the wealthy up in the hills. Here the houses were in view of the street, dating from an era when the rich would have had an army of servants as a buffer against the outside world rather than high fences and armed guards.

The Kawada house was large by 1950s

standards, maybe, but it wasn't twenty-first-century McMansion huge. Slater assessed it as he rolled past, parking farther up the block and walking back. The lawn was even and green and remarkably free of crabgrass. Just under the ground-floor windows was a lush and neatly trimmed *Podocarpus* that someone obviously knew how to take care of, and he admired the work that had gone into it as he rang the bell.

A guy in his twenties with a shock of coiffed jet-black hair answered the door. He looked a little like Steve, lean and athletic, with the same square jaw. He was probably older than he looked, Slater decided, like other Japanese people he'd met. Given the opportunity, he'd totally fuck this guy.

"Can I help you?" he asked.

Like Steve, he was completely guileless, speaking politely, openly. Slater had only ever seen that in people who'd never had to struggle to get by. That alone wasn't a good enough reason to want to sucker punch him, he reminded himself.

"I'm looking for Lillian Kawada. I work for Cudahy Mutual," Slater said, handing the guy his business card.

"About the necklace?" he asked, glancing at it.

"Correct."

"She's not here."

"Steve said she'd be around today," Slater said,

raising his voice. "So who's screwing with me—him, or her, or you?"

"She just went out for lunch," he said quickly, his eyebrows shooting up. "She should be back any minute. You can wait for her, if you want."

"I will," Slater said, and followed him inside.

Beyond the foyer, the front room had a high ceiling with dark wooden beams running across it, the furniture clustered in the middle and wide windows and bookshelves around the walls. At one end, on the dark wooden floor, sat a set of dramatic gold-leaf folding screens, one depicting a trio of cranes in flight, the other reeds growing in a marsh.

"Nice place," Slater said.

"My dad always says 'I worked hard for it.' I guess he got a lot of pushback moving into the neighborhood." He scowled and lowered his voice, mimicking Steve: "'Guys who look like us didn't use to be allowed to live around here, son.' I guess that applies to guys who look like you too."

"Yeah, well, I'm glad that's changed."

In reality Slater had been in lots of houses like this one, and his mother had grown up in a similar old-money neighborhood. But the guy was right—this wasn't the world Slater inhabited.

"Are you Lillian's son?" Slater asked.

A flash of annoyance crossed his face. "No—she's my dad's new wife."

"So Steve is your dad, and she's your step-mother."

"Technically, I suppose. She hasn't been around that long, and I certainly don't need any mothering."

Slater put his hands on his hips. "What's your name, son?"

He laughed. "You're not that much older than me. It's Jeff."

He had a nice smile, almost disarming, Slater thought. "Were you there when the necklace disappeared?"

Jeff held out his palms. "I don't know anything about that. I wasn't even in the state."

"OK," Slater said, eyeing him. "So what's Lillian like?"

He sank onto the arm of an easy chair. "I'd have to say she's damaged."

"Cognitively disabled, or brain damaged?" Slater asked, frowning. "Or do you mean she's an emotional wreck?"

Jeff waved his arm. "You know, just—damaged."

"Give me an example."

"She's irrational." His brow furrowed in thought. "She has a thing with chocolate. You can't have it around her."

"You mean it upsets her to see it, or she eats it when she sees it?"

"It's a thing, right?" Jeff said, gesturing wildly, his voice rising. "You can't leave it around."

Slater watched him, wondering if Jeff might be the one who's damaged. "So what do you do?" he asked.

"I'm in graduate school, back east. Anthropology."

"You're on a break?"

"I'm supposed to be writing, but it's slow." He held Slater's gaze—for a fraction of a second too long, Slater realized. He knew that look, knew what it meant.

"I like those pants," Slater said. "They're flattering."

"Thanks," Jeff said, looking down at them, his face reddening.

"Does Steve's factory make those?"

He shook his head. "Dad only does women's wear." After a moment he added, "You don't look like a fashion victim. I'm surprised you're interested in what I'm wearing."

"You have that thing going on," Slater said, gesturing vaguely.

"What thing?"

"That effortless hotness. Clothes are only part of it."

"So that's the way it is." Jeff laughed and slapped his thigh. "I had a feeling about you."

"Anthropological insight?"

"Probably. You're too well put together to be straight. Do you want a drink?"

"It's a little early for me," Slater said. "Plus it might be hard to explain to Lillian why I'm boozing with you."

"Right." His eyes narrowed. "That's actually a good call."

"It doesn't mean we can't be friendly."

"Damn—you really are into me," Jeff said. "I'm kind of amazed. Guys like you never come after me."

"I find that hard to believe."

Jeff chuckled and stood up, approaching him. Slater admired the bulge in the fabric of his pants. Why did lanky guys always look like they had big dicks? He stopped a few inches in front of Slater, so close that he could feel Jeff's breath.

"You should check out the fabric," Jeff said, holding his gaze. "It's really luxe."

Slater reached out and grabbed the belt loops on either side, pulling Jeff against him. Surprised and laughing, Jeff went with it, putting his hands on Slater's waist.

"You don't mess around," Jeff said, and then, "whoa—you're warm."

"In my business that's usually considered a good sign."

"Are you going to kiss me?"

Slater obliged, leaning in to meet his eager

mouth, exploring it. The guy was too tentative and stiff, but still, Slater felt himself getting hard.

"You've got a stiffy," Jeff said, leaning into him.

"What are we going to do about that?"

The front door rattled in the foyer, followed by the sound of it swinging open.

Jeff pulled away. "Nothing—that's Lillian." He stepped across the room, adjusting the front of his pants.

Slater shifted his satchel and held it in front of his jeans. "My number's on my card. Call me before nine, and we'll finish this."

"Why nine?" Jeff said, standing across the room, still flushed.

"That's when I start drinking, and I won't be able to perform if I'm loaded."

Jeff cocked his head quizzically, but turned away as Lillian came in.

The woman had gravity, tacitly demanding attention when she entered the room, her presence taking up much more space than her diminutive frame alone. Her hair was black and cut pixie-short, with large earrings that sparkled on both sides, and she wore a pink sweater set with a dark skirt, three strands of pearls draped below her collar. It seemed like a lot of bling for a lunch outing.

"This is Slater," Jeff said, as Lillian stopped and eyed them both. "He's from the insurance company, to talk about your necklace."

"Steve said you were going to drop by," she said, with careful, measured enunciation, the product of a pricey education, or maybe just the aspiration to that social stratum. "Have you been waiting long?"

"Jeff has been entertaining me," Slater said.

Jeff blushed again, and a smirk played on Lillian's lips.

"You have nice things," Slater continued, nodding to the gilded folding screens. "Are those Japanese?"

Lillian waved a languorous hand. "Probably. My parents were born here, so I'm about as Japanese as you are. My decorator picked them. I do know that they're expensive."

"Of course they're Japanese," Jeff said, frowning at her, and to Slater, "My dad is proud of our heritage."

Not masking her annoyance with Jeff, Lillian turned to Slater, her eyes flicking down to his jeans and his boots. "What do you do for the insurance company? You don't look like you work in an office."

"Research," Slater said, and handed her his card.

"Field investigator," she read, and scowled. "What are you investigating?"

"I need you to give me an account of what happened the night the necklace went missing."

"It was stolen," she said firmly, holding his

gaze. "I've sung that tune in every key, Mr. Ibáñez."

"What do you mean by that?"

"I already told the police all about it—answered all their questions."

"I'm not the police."

"Fine," she said flatly, and waved to a chair.

Slater pulled off his satchel, his woody having subsided, and took out his tablet. Lillian went to one end of the sofa. Watching her sit down, she seemed impatient, but not cognitively impaired. Maybe the damage Jeff had spoken of was emotional. Slater took the adjacent wing chair, and Jeff perched on the arm of the easy chair across the room, too far to be part of the conversation but close enough to hear what was said, as if he were torn between leaving and listening in.

"What do you need to know?" Lillian asked.

As he spoke, Slater met her eye but manipulated his tablet to snap a surreptitious photo of her. "Why were you at the factory? You don't work there."

"I don't work at all," she said, raising her eyebrows. "I was trying on a gown. Steve makes clothes, so I get all the custom couture I want."

"Why did you have such an expensive piece of jewelry with you?"

"We were going to the opera."

"Oh," Slater said, raising his eyebrows. "I'm sorry."

Jeff chuckled, but Lillian ignored him. "Excuse me?"

"You were going by choice?" Slater asked.

"Yes," she said slowly, as if he weren't too bright. "The factory is on the way. I took off the necklace, set it on the table, and pulled the curtain to change."

"Is that the only jewelry you had on?"

"I didn't have to take off my earrings for a fitting."

"So you're changing clothes," Slater said, scribbling notes on his tablet.

"It wasn't more than two or three minutes, and it was gone. We called the police right away."

He looked up at her. "Who else was there?"

"Steve, of course, and his office clerk, or whatever she is."

"Carolina. Anyone else?"

Lillian looked thoughtful. "I think some of the garment workers were still there—I remember the police questioning one of them. I don't remember their names."

That didn't ring true, Slater thought, watching her. Most victims would have been keenly aware of anyone who might have perpetrated the theft.

"Did you see anyone else?" he asked. "Someone who admired the necklace in the parking lot, maybe, or in the elevator?"

"Anyone could have walked in off the street,"

she said intently. "I know that sounds foolish, but I didn't think there was any risk. I didn't see anyone because I was inside the curtain, and everyone else had their backs turned."

"What about that accounting thing?" Jeff said.

Lillian shot him a look, barely perceptibly shaking her head.

"What accounting thing?" Slater demanded.

"It's nothing," Lillian said. "No connection."

"OK," Slater said, and eyed Jeff, silent now, and added to his notes:

find out about the accounting thing

"So who do you think took it?" he asked, again meeting Lillian's gaze.

"I've no idea," she snapped, anger flashing in her eyes, but just as quickly, she suppressed it.

"What's the best way to get hold of you?"

"My cell, I suppose." She sighed and recited the number. "Will the reimbursement be delayed by your inquiries?"

"My work is part of the process. I'm not sure what the office told you in terms of a timeline." He was obfuscating, of course, as the desk jockeys would wait as long as it took for Slater to report back to them.

She watched him for a moment before speaking. "I don't really understand what you're investigating. It's all completely straightforward."

"Still, I have to get a clear picture of what happened, and talk to the people who were there." Tucking his tablet away, he rose and slung his satchel onto his shoulder.

Lillian rose with him, absently smoothing her skirt.

"I'll be in touch," he told her, and on his way to the foyer, shot Jeff a louche wink, eliciting another blush.

Walking out to the street, he could feel eyes on him. Maybe it was just Jeff, checking out the fit of his jeans, or it could be Lillian—her reactions seemed authentic, and appropriate, given the circumstances. She was suspicious of Slater, naturally enough, as his queries were delaying her payout. Still, something about her was off.

Driving home, his phone rang, with a ring tone that instantly made his heart sink: *No wire hangers, ever! I buy you beautiful dresses, and you treat them like they were some dishrag ...*"

"I'm working, Doris," he answered, exasperated.

"I'm glad to hear that. You know, I think this climate change thing is making my bougainvillea go crazy. It's still winter and it looks like a jungle out there."

"So hire a gardener. Or ask your stupid boyfriend to cut it back."

She laughed. "Albert doesn't know anything

about horticulture. You planted them—I thought you'd know best how to manage them. Maybe you could take a little break and drop by. You're so good at it. It'll only take you a few minutes."

Slater sighed loudly, for her benefit. "Only a Jewish mother could induce a guilt trip from across town."

"Well, I'm not Catholic, or Tamil, so a Jewish mother is what you get."

"I'll swing by if I have time," he said, and ended the call.

Slater managed to live his life mostly free of obligations to people, except for her and Conrad. At least Conrad had some utility. He wanted Doris to move away, to some little town up the coast, like a normal retiree. "I can't afford to do that," she protested, pointing out that she was living on a teacher's pension. Almost anywhere else was cheaper than LA, he'd explained, but so far she showed no sign of budging.

Kawada Couture would have to wait. Nosing the Thunderbird into the alley, he parked in his garage and went upstairs, setting his satchel on the kitchen counter and fishing out Steve Kawada's card. He punched the cell number into his phone and texted him:

> I can't drop by today. Does tomorrow morning
> work for you and Carolina?

By the time he'd changed into a heavy work shirt, Steve had replied:

At your leisure, good sir.

The guy was such a softy. If everyone were so artless, so amenable, Slater would be out of a job. Stuffing his phone in his jeans, he went into the bathroom and spent a few minutes shaving. If he was going to see Doris, he had no choice.

Down in the garage, he looked through his tools—the gardening stuff hanging on the wall, not the Russian surveillance gear, which was locked in the armored cabinet past the nose of the Thunderbird. He already had a shovel in the trunk, as anyone in his business should, and a pair of work gloves, but if he was going to be tangling with thorny bougainvillea, he needed a heavier pair, the gauntlets, along with the hedge trimmer. Doris's roses would undoubtedly need pruning— it was that time of year—so he loaded both sets of shears into the trunk with everything else.

Navigating to Doris's street in hilly Mount Washington took a while on the perpetually congested 110 through downtown, even though it wasn't very far. As he drove up her block, far- ther along he spotted another dramatic magnolia, its riot of huge pink flowers seemingly floating above the sidewalk.

Any pleasure he felt at that early sign of spring

was squelched by the sight of her boyfriend's stupid little Boxster, parked in the driveway with the top up. Why would you get a convertible if you're not going to leave the top down? It had been raining, admittedly, but still—what a freaking moron. Doris's Buick was gone, and he scowled as he pulled up behind the Boxster and shifted into Park. She wouldn't dare leave him alone to deal with Albert. If she had, Albert was going to get coldcocked.

But Doris was home when he banged on the door, opening it to greet him. Petite and shorter than her son, she was letting the gray show in her hair these days. Reaching up to embrace him, she planted a kiss on his newly clean-shaven cheek.

"Where's your car?" Slater demanded.

"Albert's wasn't running right, and he was afraid it was going to conk out, so he borrowed mine."

"That's how it starts. Next he'll want power of attorney, and drain all your bank accounts."

Doris scoffed, waving her hand. "He has his own money—he doesn't need mine."

"You know that Porsche made tanks for the Nazis, right?"

"Albert's not a Nazi," she said emphatically, grabbing his forearm and giving it a squeeze.

"Still, it's insensitive. What self-respecting grown-up drives around in a doll car?"

"I know what you're doing," she said. "You're being protective of me. You think you should be the only man in my life."

"I'm the only one that I trust."

"That's what your ex said."

"What?" Slater snapped. "Have you been hanging out with him? Did you two take a spinning class?"

She frowned. "Why would I do that? We just talked on the phone."

"Treachery, Doris. Treachery and betrayal."

"No one is betraying you," she said, exasperated. "Conrad is a nice guy, and I'm allowed to have relationships with people without your permission."

"Not with him."

"Well, suck it up. It's not about you, anyway."

That was a lie, Slater knew. Of course it was all about him. There was no other reason they'd talk.

Stifling his retort and turning back to the door, he said, "I'm going to hit the bougainvillea."

Lifting the trunk lid and pulling on the gauntlets, he carried his tools through the side gate into the backyard. A hedge of bougainvillea ran the entire length of one side, along the fence line, and it was indeed in need of trimming, with leafy runners sprouting at crazy angles, reaching for the sun. The roses on the other side of the yard needed work too. He'd planted all of them when he'd worked in horticulture after high school, when Doris had managed to get him into a community college program with a lot of physical labor, probably in an attempt to give him an outlet for his aggression. The hard work had felt good then, and he enjoyed it now, sculpting the hedge back into a sensible form, although the electric hedge trimmer did most of the heavy lifting.

He spent the time required to shape it evenly, getting the top right, snagging the stray runners. The roses took a lot longer, pruning the individual branches with their stubborn thorns. Finally he cut up all the detritus and raked it together, stuffed it in the green can, then took a look around the yard. The effort had made him sweaty and tired, but it was worth it—the place looked tight, and it wouldn't need work again until spring. After he lugged his tools back to his car, he went inside, where Doris had sandwiches waiting for them on the dining table.

"I used your fake mayo, and fake turkey," she said as they sat down.

"Thanks for doing that. You can just call it vegan mayo and vegan turkey, if you want."

As they ate, Doris gazed out at the backyard. "It always looks so bleak after you do that to the roses."

"But in the spring, they go nuts," he said. "You love that part."

"I guess I just hate this time of year. The long shadows make it feel like dusk all day, and it gets dark so early."

"We used to call it the balance of the seasons. Getting through the dark depths of winter means we can really value the warmer months."

"Listen to you," she said. "My son, the philosopher."

After they'd eaten, Doris took his empty plate and stacked it on her own. "Do you want to take a shower?"

"I'll do that at home."

"Hot date tonight?"

"That's none of your business," he said irritably.

"It's OK to take things slowly once in a while. You don't have to jump into bed with every guy you meet."

"My god, woman—I am not going to talk about my sex life with you."

"When you're sober, at least," she said, raising an eyebrow.

Slater folded his arms and glared at her. "Did Conrad tell you that?"

"I'm just saying—a man isn't going to want to buy the cow when he can get the milk for free."

"That's it," Slater said, pulling his napkin out of his lap and dropping it on the table. "I'm out."

Doris followed him to the front door. "Thanks

for all the hard work, sweetie."

Slater turned and stooped to kiss her. "Love you," he said, and straightening up, "Stop talking to Conrad."

"That's none of your business," she said cheerfully.

Slater pushed open the screen door and stepped outside. "And tell Albert to buy a real car. It's embarrassing."

Driving home, he could feel a knot in his stomach thinking about what she'd implied. What had he told her about his sex life when he wasn't sober? He had no memory of anything like that. Maybe it was a Conrad back-channel, and he'd told her something gossipy. Despite their denials, it felt like they were plotting against him.

At home he showered and put on a T-shirt and sweat pants, then stretched out on the sofa, turning on the radio news. It was nothing that he gave a damn about, just filler, but soon enough it would switch to music.

Waking to his phone ringing, he scrabbled in the darkness, finding it on the carpet. It was a 213 number, without a name attached, but he knew who it was, and it made him grin. Killing the radio, he answered, "Ibáñez."

"Hi—so, um, we met earlier today."

"I remember you, Jeff."

"Right." He laughed nervously. "We talked about getting together."

"You can come over here," Slater said, "or I can come to you."

"I'm staying with my dad and Lillian right now, so it's not a good place for a booty call."

Slater chuckled. "Is that what your frat brothers call it?"

"I wasn't in a frat."

"I'll text you my address, but I'll warn you, my apartment is not pretty."

"What's wrong with it?"

"Think of your house," Slater said, "and then imagine the polar opposite of that, in every regard. Small instead of big, dark instead of sunny, grungy instead of clean."

"I'm sure I can handle it—I'm going to school in New York."

"I'll be here," Slater said, and ended the call, then texted his address, adding:

Take a ride-share. There's nowhere to park.

There wasn't much to tidy up, but he put the bourbon out of sight in the cupboard, and picked up the laundry strewn around his bedroom, dumping it in the bottom of the closet. Before long there was a tentative knock at the door.

When Jeff came in, he awkwardly kissed Slater, half on the mouth, half on the cheek.

"You shaved," he exclaimed, and then looked around the room. "You weren't kidding. This place is rough as guts."

"Thank you," Slater said, hands on his hips. "So what are you into, Jeff?"

"You mean sex?" he said, turning to him. "I don't sleep around a lot. I mean, I don't really know what I'm doing."

"You could have fooled me, when I was at your house—you seemed pretty confident."

"I guess I get by." He took a deep breath. "So what are my options?"

Slater had to grin. "That's up to you. What turns you on? You want to cuddle with Dad, or get plowed, or get smacked around?"

"I've already got a dad, so not that," he said. "I kind of love the way your body looks. Maybe we could just get naked and go from there."

"That, I can do," Slater said, and led him into the bedroom.

"Sweet—a futon," Jeff said. "You know, the ones in Japan are totally different. The floor itself is kind of the mattress. It's made of straw."

"Lillian implied you were third generation," Slater said, untying his sweatpants and stepping out of them.

"It doesn't mean I haven't been there," Jeff said absently, focusing now on Slater's naked body. "So where do you want me?"

"Come here," Slater said, and when Jeff approached, turned him around, wrapping his arms around his chest, sliding them slowly over his shirt, then underneath it, feeling his belly and his chest. Jeff leaned into him, and unbuttoned his shirt. Slater pulled him onto the bed, and soon both of them were naked. At first Slater cuddled with him, focusing on the feeling of warm skin, but eventually shifted to Jeff's rock-hard cock, stroking it, and then working his fingers inside him.

"I'm going to fuck you," Slater said softly in his ear.

He rolled on a condom and slid gently into him, taking his time, then increasing the rhythm. Jeff moaned with the intensity, his eyes screwed shut. With his nose buried in Jeff's thick hair, Slater came, thrusting deeper, then pulled out, his hand on Jeff's cock, stroking it and kissing his neck until he came too, groaning and arching his back.

After Jeff caught his breath, he said, "Nice."

Slater murmured assent, glad that was all he had to say, that he didn't need to process it, or deliver a monologue—lucky for Slater, Jeff wasn't the chatty type. With quiet, he could think his own thoughts. The booze was waiting, he knew, sitting patiently in the cupboard, golden and constant—but not yet.

He climbed out of bed to ditch the condom and wash his hands in the kitchen sink. Opening the cupboard, he pulled out the bourbon. Fuck it, he decided—one drink wouldn't hurt, and he took a long pull from the bottle. Jeff passed behind him on his way to the bathroom, and Slater went back to the futon, flicking off the room lights; enough illumination was diffusing in from the kitchen. He put his arm over his eyes, but felt Jeff climb into bed again, lying close, his arm draped over Slater's chest.

"Jack Daniels?" Jeff asked.

"Close. Jim Beam."

Jeff chuckled. "The frat boys at my school drank Jack."

Slater moved his arm and turned to look at him in the dim light. "What were you talking about today when you said Lillian had some accounting thing?"

"It wasn't her. Dad's company had an incident a couple of months ago. I wondered if it might be connected. I think Lillian didn't want me to tell you about it because Dad is embarrassed. I certainly would be. He tells me all this company stuff because he wants me to be interested in the business. I'm totally not, though—I don't want to be his partner, or his successor."

"He knows that, and he hasn't cut you off?"

"Financially? Of course not. He's not a tyrant."

"You're a lucky man," Slater said. "What was the accounting incident?"

"Dad has this firm that does his taxes. They come in a few times a year and go through the books. One day this woman shows up when he's not there and convinces Carolina she's one of the accountants. Carolina lets her get on a computer and opens the books. A couple of days later they realize she's drained the current account."

"How did she manage that?"

"I don't know the details, or how much she got, but I think it was a significant amount—there was a lot of anguish, let me tell you. I'm not even sure if Dad called the cops. I haven't heard anything about it lately."

"How did she convince Carolina she was legit?"

Jeff rolled onto his back and interlaced his hand with Slater's thick fingers, resting them on his chest. "He said this woman gave Carolina a business card, and mentioned the two accountants who usually come by name. Carolina fell for it."

"Why is Carolina still working for him?"

"She's been there forever, and my dad is a people person. He wants everyone to be happy. It wasn't her fault, he said—anyone could have been tricked that way."

"Do you remember what her name was, this

con artist, or what Carolina said she looked like?"

"Ask Carolina," Jeff said. "I'm sure she'll never forget."

It didn't sound like it was connected, Slater thought, and it was unlikely that a grifter would have come back to do a snatch-and-run, especially at just the right moment to steal something no one except Lillian would have known was going to be there. Still, it was interesting—the perp came by on a day when Steve wasn't around, and that probably wasn't by chance.

"Lillian seems kind of materialistic," Slater said.

"That's all she is," Jeff said. "She has no depth, or intellect, or curiosity about the world. There's nothing warm about her, or caring, except when she fakes it to get what she wants. But she is efficient."

"Damaged," Slater offered.

"Exactly. You should see her in her natural environment. It's so obvious what's going on."

"What is going on?"

Jeff sighed. "I think she's a chiseler. She doesn't love my dad; she loves his resources."

"Do you think Steve knows that?"

"He's smart, so he's probably entertained the idea, at least. I'm sure he'd rather it wasn't true."

"What did you mean by her natural environment?"

"They belong to this country club. It's nowhere near the country—it's in Koreatown, a few blocks from where they live. I guess it's more like a spa. My dad pays for it and never goes, but Lillian practically lives there. There's tennis and a swimming pool, and lots of rich people sitting on their butts and gossiping."

"What's the place called?" Slater asked, gently massaging Jeff's hand with his thumb as he talked.

"The Kensington Club. She's there every day."

"What time every day?"

"Before lunch, and she dines there sometimes. Are you going to drop in?"

"You said I should see her in her native element."

"She's going to be so pissed," Jeff said. In the low light, Slater could see him grinning at the thought.

"So what was that thing about the opera?" Jeff asked.

"What are you talking about?"

"Lillian said they were going to the opera, and you asked if she was going by choice. It was funny."

"Right—I was just winding her up. In my business, sometimes you get a more honest reaction if you provoke people a little."

"Interesting. I guess she didn't take the bait."

"In a way, she did," Slater said, disengaging his hand and rubbing his nose with his palm. "She looked at me like I was a philistine, not even smart enough to understand the value of opera. That tells me a lot about her."

"So you were feeling her out. Do you think she's trying to scam your company?"

"I'm not sure."

Jeff was quiet for a while, then said, "You have an unusual job. What did you surmise about me?"

"That you're a smoking-hot little fucker."

He laughed. "I'll take it."

Slater got up and went to the kitchen, taking several long pulls of bourbon, closing his eyes and relishing the burn.

"You're welcome to sleep here," he told Jeff when he got back to bed, "but there's nothing to eat."

"I smell booze again. Did you ever think you might have a drinking problem?"

"Why would I think that? I'm completely in control of what I drink." Slater grinned to himself, feeling the golden wave washing over him. He didn't care what the guy said, and relaxed into the sensation of his muscles unwinding, the warmth in his belly that was pushing his consciousness downward.

"If you say so," Jeff said. "So why do you live in this place? It's kind of a dump."

"I told you about that before you came over, princess," he said, his tongue growing thick as his mind sank toward sleep. "I'm not who you think I am."

Whatever else Jeff had to say was lost to Slater as he slid into the sweet dizzy buzz of unconsciousness.

The guy was gone when he woke up, and Slater took his time to get to full speed before he reached for his phone. It was still early. He hadn't drunk that much, so it was painless to climb out of bed, except for the cold air. After he peed, he looked in the fridge and drank the last of the orange juice, throwing out the bottle, and then sat in his recliner to look at his phone.

His calendar reminded him that Rosa, his cleaner, was coming at ten. He definitely wanted to be out of here by then. This place was too small to stay, or to hang around and supervise like a bored suburbanite. There was nothing she'd want to steal anyway; the only expensive stuff he had was the Russian surveillance gear, and that was locked up in the armored cabinet in his garage or in the safe at the office.

Max had left him a voice message, and he read the transcript: "Hey, bud, I'm on a window-shade job today. I might be in the office later. Call me if you need me."

It was sweet that he thought Slater would give a damn about what he was doing, but he knew what it was—that thing a shrink had once tried to teach him, about dealing with other people. "Bridge building," she'd called it, building a rapport. In this case, him and Max creating their business partnership.

Slater didn't envy him that work, trying to catch cheating spouses in the act. In the old days it actually did involve peeping around window shades, but these days the surveillance was more likely to happen in a hotel. That made it a lot easier. It was weird that people thought they had privacy at hotels—they were very public places, usually with cameras and always with lots of eye-balls. He texted Max:

Chasing jewelry for Della today. Have fun.

Checking the time, he saw he had to get moving, and pulled on his jeans and boots and one of the last clean shirts in his closet. A while back, Rosa had pitied him enough to expand her job description to include doing his laundry. It was worth the extra dough he paid her—now he never had to wear a dirty shirt. He left Rosa's cash on the kitchen counter and trotted down the two flights to the garage.

The Kensington Club was a short drive, his phone told him, and he soon found it on a leafy backstreet. From the front it looked like an old hotel, and rather than stopping at the valet, he parked farther up the block. The expansive lobby was dominated by a long counter, staffed by a man and a woman, both wearing casual white uniforms. They looked like spa employees, not security, but the layout of the place gave them that role—there was no way in except past them. As he approached, the woman gave him the once over.

"Can I help you?" she asked.

"I have a meeting with Lillian Kawada," Slater said.

The clerk nodded, and pointed to the side door. "She's out by the pool, past the bar."

Slater was surprised that she'd bought his story, that she didn't check it with Lillian, but he didn't hesitate, nodding thanks and walking in. Maybe this club wasn't all that exclusive, or maybe he didn't look as out of place as he assumed he would in denim.

The club's outdoor space had luxuriant fussy landscaping—cycads and staghorns, even canaria palms; those were crazy expensive. The bar was on the left, a rattan-fronted island amid the foliage, and beyond it were café tables and chaises longues arrayed around the pool. Oddly it wasn't very blue, as pools usually were, surfaced with some kind of tile that gave it lightness and texture beneath the placid surface. No one was swimming, or lounging on the chaises, which was unsurprising, given the coolness of the morning.

Several of the tables were occupied, however, and scanning them, the back of a woman's head caught his eye—Lillian. Those were the sparkly earrings he'd seen yesterday. She was with two other women, one at either elbow, and all of them looked upscale, dressed for the weather, one with a yellow scarf at her neck, the other with a plaid-lined overcoat falling open and chic gray streaks in her dark hair.

There was no music, just the sound of conversations and the tinkle of water in a fountain somewhere amid the greenery—if he sat at the bar, he should be able to overhear Lillian and her friends. Surprisingly, given how early it was, a young woman with Caribbean-braided hair, a white shirt, and a black bowtie was tending bar, even though no one was sitting here. The moment Slater slid onto a stool she stepped over to him.

"OJ," Slater said quietly, and cocked his head to listen to the nearby table. There were other conversations going on, but if he concentrated, he could make out everything Lillian and her friends were saying.

The bartender set down a highball glass in front of him, and he reached into his pants pocket for his cash.

"How much?" he asked her.

"It's complimentary," she said, and stepped away.

The one in the yellow scarf was talking. "*She has no idea how to access those places. You have to make the connections first. You can't just show up on the doorstep.*" As he listened, he figured out that they were bemoaning a friend's incompetence in finding a school for her kid, couched in sober concern for her well-being when really they were just trash-talking her.

By the time he'd drunk most of his orange juice, Slater was debating whether to leave, as the conversation was mind-numbingly boring and not at all informative. He watched a woman in a bathrobe come out of the main building, then stop on the opposite side of the bar and order a Bellini. After she served her, the bartender came back to Slater.

"More OJ?"

"Sure," he said, and pushed the glass toward her, stifling a yawn.

The conversation turned to finance, with gray-streaks explaining what a short sale was, and how to make money from it. It would be surprising if these women did their own investing; rich folks usually had staff or brokers for that purpose. Maybe they were just discussing it out of interest. Lillian seemed to be listening more than talking, but finally gray-streaks changed the subject.

"Has insurance paid you yet for that lovely necklace? It was such a tragic loss."

Slater glanced sidelong at them, seeing Lillian lean forward.

"They're being quite petty about it. I've done all the paperwork, and the police report too. I assume it's a lot of money for them to just dash off a check. It's not like it's a dented fender."

Yellow-scarf tittered. "I only saw you wear it once, but it was so dramatic. What is it worth, if you don't mind me asking?"

"Half a million, easily," Lillian said. "I had it custom designed, but I know the stones have gone up in value."

Gray-streaks pushed her glass away. "It's time for my Reiki class," she said, and air-kissed both of them before walking toward the main building.

Yellow-scarf rose with her. "I should be off too. I'm getting my eyes lasered today."

Slipping off the barstool, Slater approached Lillian, still sitting at the little table as her friends left. She looked surprised at first, and then her eyes narrowed.

"What are you doing here?"

"I had some follow-up questions about your claim," Slater said, hands on his hips.

"And you thought it was appropriate to crash my social club?"

"You had the necklace insured for a hundred and seventy-five thousand, but you just told your friends it was worth a lot more."

"Were you eavesdropping on me?" she demanded, angry now.

"I overheard you. You're in a public place."

"How did you get in here, anyway?" And louder, "This is a private club."

Slater frowned. "You do realize that I'm the man with the money, right? If I have to report that you're being uncooperative, your claim could drag on for months. Maybe years."

Lillian considered that, glaring at him, and then glanced around. "Sit down," she said, and picked up her champagne flute, sipping at its orangey-pink contents.

She was drinking a Bellini too, Slater thought, dropping into the chair where yellow-scarf had been.

"So which is it?" he demanded. "One seventy-five, or half a mil?"

She sighed. "Of course it was underinsured. Steve had to keep the premiums reasonable, and I never expected to have it stolen. It's probably not worth five hundred thousand," she said, eyeing him, "but there's no law against exaggerating a story with your friends."

"I get it. You're competing with Reiki and laser surgery."

Lillian smiled coyly, dropping her chin and holding his gaze. "I bet you don't have to exaggerate, do you."

Slater stared at her. The transition from impatient and businesslike to femme fatale was so rapid that it took a moment to process. Maybe this was the damage Jeff had talked about.

"Are you flirting with me right now?" he said.

"That depends," she said, her eyes wide and dewy, flicking down to his chest and back again, a classic romantic salvo. "Is it working?"

"Doesn't Steve keep you satisfied? He's very good-looking."

Lillian scoffed, instantly dropping the coquette and looking away. "Let's just say he's a good earner."

"What about Jeff? How do you get along with him?"

"Jeff is stupid."

Slater frowned. "He's a graduate student. He can't be that stupid."

"He's book smart," she said, waving impatiently, "but lots of poor people are book smart. His father offered him a giant pearl on the half-shell, sitting on a red velvet pillow, and he spit on it."

"You mean he doesn't want to go into the family business."

"He's being ridiculous. It's a hugely profitable entity." She shifted in her chair. "In any case, it's not my concern. What does Jeff have to do with my insurance claim?"

"I'm not sure yet," he said, and rose, heading toward the entrance. In the lobby he nodded to the desk clerk, then headed out to the street.

Once he got downtown, he parked in the lot across from his building, then walked the few blocks to Kawada Couture. A woman cutting fabric at a table facing the elevator eyed him as he came in, calling out *"Patrón."* Despite Steve's dismissal of the need for security, it seemed the workers, at least, were wary of interlopers.

Steve rose from his desk and greeted Slater like an old friend. Slater's instinct was to fix that with a quick left hook, but he knew Steve wasn't deliberately trying to piss him off.

"Are you always in such a good mood?" Slater demanded.

Steve laughed, as if it were a joke. "I'm thinking you're here to see Carolina."

"That was the plan."

"She'll be back any minute."

"What about Faith, is she here?"

'She's out all week, I'm afraid," he said, folding

his arms, then grinning affably. "So how did you get into the insurance racket?"

Like an older version of Jeff, he really did have a nice smile, Slater had to admit, once he'd decided it wasn't meant to provoke him. Still, it didn't mean he wasn't up to something.

"Someone told me I'm good with people," Slater said.

Steve looked toward the elevator. "Here she is."

Slater turned to see Carolina walking in, her hair tamer now than when she'd been out drinking, but still eye-catching and voluminous. Today she wore a smart black suit tailored to accentuate her curves.

Steve stepped toward her and introduced Slater.

"I guess you want to ask me about the robbery," she said, concern in her eyes. "That was a really terrible night. If I'd looked up from my computer, even for a second, I might have caught the thief. Lillian was so distraught."

"Was there anything else that day that felt wrong?" Slater asked. "Nobody had guests drop in, for example?"

She shook her head slowly. "Nothing like that."

"What about the accounting scam? Do you think there's any connection?"

"I can't imagine there would be," she said, startled. "That woman wouldn't be foolish enough to show up here again."

"What was her name?" Slater asked.

"Silvana Lee," she said, and spelled it, looking away. "At least according to her business card."

Slater pulled out his tablet and wrote down the name. As he looked up, he tilted the device and snapped a surreptitious photo of her.

"Do you still have the card?" he asked.

"I gave it to the police. The accounting firm said it was fake anyway."

"How do you know about that incident?" Steve asked, furrowing his brow. "The police wouldn't have told you. Was it Lillian? She said you were chatting with Jeff. Did he tell you?"

"It's my job to dig up this stuff," Slater said.

"You don't need to be asking Jeff about my business. You ask me. He's not the least bit interested in the company."

It was the first sign of true ire he'd seen in Steve, and it made Slater grin. "Jeff is a college boy, he told me."

"Ever since he went away to school and came out, he's been quite the independent thinker," Steve said. "He left here my son, and came back gay."

"Not that those are mutually incompatible," Slater said pointedly.

"Of course not. But I built this business with my bare hands. Now that he's out, he won't even show his face here. It's like he's too good for us."

Slater scoffed. "I know lots of gay guys who'd be in hog heaven to have their own clothing factory."

"You're conflating gay with growing up," Carolina said to Steve. "He's a man now, and he doesn't want to be part of your business. The grass is always greener, right?"

"Still, he's studying anthropology," Steve said. "What kind of job is that going to get him? Sitting on a riverbank in the rainforest communing with Stone Age people?"

"He'll find a career," she said, "or maybe he won't. Maybe he'll walk in here one day and ask for a job. Either way, him coming out is incidental to all of it."

Steve sighed. "I know you're right." To Slater, he grinned and said, "You see why I keep her around? She's like half my brain."

"What did she look like?" Slater asked Carolina.

"Silvana Lee?" she said, her face clouding. "Very glamorous. Lots of hair and an inch of pancake makeup, with that definition shading like drag queens use."

That was an interesting observation, coming from someone who wore a lot of makeup too, someone he'd seen at a drag show. He assessed her as her jotted notes. Carolina could easily pass for a drag queen.

"Blond, brunette?" Slater asked.

"She was Asian, but with a lot of blond in her hair, and she wore those blue contacts. You know how those just look weird? You can't help but notice they're fake."

"Height, weight?"

"About like me," she said, "and on the thin side. She was wearing a sharp suit—the hemline was almost up to her *chalupa*. There's video."

"Can I see it?" he said, irritated that she hadn't mentioned that first.

Carolina looked to Steve.

"Sure—we have a copy," Steve said. "It's from the camera in the lobby."

"At least it works some of the time," Slater said.

Steve chuckled and went to his desk, digging through folders on his computer with Slater peering over his shoulder. Carolina stood back by a work table, arms folded, not watching.

The video was a distorted wide-angle view of the lobby, in black and white, with a date stamp running in the top corner. The center of the image, where the building's front entrance should be, was a white blob, overexposed from the daylight flooding in. A fuzzy dark shape appeared in the blob and then stepped out of it, discernible only for a few seconds as a person walking into the building toward the elevators. It was a woman in a short skirt with voluminous hair, holding a thin bag or a briefcase in one hand and a manila folder in the other, held up to her forehead to completely obscure her face. She took three steps and was gone.

"She knew about the camera," Slater said. "That means she also knew you didn't have any surveillance up here."

"It seems like she was well prepared," Steve said, looking up at him.

"She's also been here before. Play it again."

Steve ran the video, and Slater looked closer, but nothing in the grainy image stood out as distinctive.

"There's a clip of when she left," Steve said, and clicked on another video file.

The view was the same, although the oversaturated blob was smaller now, later in the day. She wasn't covering her face this time, but she didn't have to, as the camera saw only the back of her head and her big hair as she took a few steps and disappeared into the blob.

He had Steve replay it and then turned to Carolina. "What color is her suit?"

"True vermilion," she said.

"What's vermilion?"

Steve answered, rising from his chair. "It's a specific color we use in the fabric business. Deeply saturated red with a hint of orange in it."

"Red," Slater said, half to himself. "So she cut a striking figure."

"She was skittish too," Carolina said. "I remember thinking that she wanted to get right to work, no small talk."

"That makes sense, considering what she was up to," Slater said.

"In hindsight, yes," Carolina said, and looked down.

"How much did Silvana get?"

Carolina winced, and Steve spoke. "I'm not going to tell you that."

"It was a lot," Carolina said, folding her arms. "I feel terrible about letting her trick me. I'll never forgive myself."

Steve put a hand on her shoulder. "It could have happened to anyone. You know that."

"Do you have a record of meetings with customers, deliveries, pickups, that kind of thing?" Slater asked.

"I keep track of all that," Carolina said.

"Can you check who came in the day the necklace was stolen? Even if it was much earlier."

Carolina's eyes flitted to Steve, who must have given tacit approval, as she said, "Follow me."

She sat at her desk, and Slater pulled over a

chair from the cutting table. Steve sat at his own desk, clicking at his computer but well within earshot.

As Carolina started tapping at her keyboard, she let Slater watch as she entered her password: "glamour girl." He scrawled it on his tablet. How could she be so lax? But Carolina was oblivious, studying the screen.

"Are those your kids?" Slater asked, pointing at the photos taped to the wall.

"Oh, no," she said, looking up. "My sister's. And that one is the boyfriend."

"Nice. He's good-looking."

"He thinks so too, unfortunately." She looked back to her screen, scrolling through a spreadsheet. "So, the day before, in the morning, the vintage fabric guy brought some product, but I've known him for years. The morning of the day it happened, we had an outgoing order to a retail store."

"With a shipping service?"

"The store is here in town," she said, "so we send a runner."

"A day laborer?"

She looked thoughtful. "I went myself. I had a lunch date on that side of town, so I dropped it off on the way."

"It wasn't a massive order, then, if you could take it in your own car."

"Small batches are all we do here," she said,

glancing into the factory. "It's basically what *couture* means these days."

"What's the name of the store?" Slater asked.

"African Goddess. It's on Robertson."

"Who's your contact there?"

"Mr. Pierre."

Slater looked up from making notes. "Is that what he calls himself?"

"Didn't he come back with part of that order?" Steve said, eyeing Carolina.

"He did. It must have been the next day." She looked back to her spreadsheet.

"No, it was the same day," Steve said slowly. "I remember thinking that he went through the order awfully quickly, because he almost beat you back here after your lunch."

"Why did he bring stuff back?" Slater asked.

"He thought there were production flaws that needed to be repaired. There weren't."

"He's one of those fussy types," Carolina added.

Slater leaned back in his chair and pursed his lips.

"Are you going to go see him?" Steve asked.

"It sounds like I have to."

Steve grinned. "Do you want to make a delivery? I have a rack of jackets for Mr. Pierre."

Slater didn't really need a cover, but it might give him a way to observe Mr. Pierre with his guard down. You could learn a lot about people by how they treated the help.

Steve led him to a rack of clothes back by the conference table, pulling out a small bundle of hangers.

"It's easy," he said. "You can carry them in one hand."

"Does someone need to sign for them?" Slater asked.

"Usually, yes. But I know you, so there's no need."

You don't actually know me, Slater thought, but he had to admit it was a reasonable bet that he wasn't going to steal a bundle of women's jackets. Scanning the room as he left, the woman cutting fabric smiled when their eyes met, but no one else seemed concerned about what he was doing.

In the elevator down, he held up the jackets for a closer look. Through the thin plastic sheeting protecting them he could see dark-blue fabric, but it was hard to tell what they were like. When he walked into his own building with the garments in hand, no one hanging around outside or in the lobby even looked at him twice. It pissed him off that they assumed he was in the trade.

Draping the jackets over his guest chair, Slater sat at his desk, waking his computer to look at the photos he'd taken over the last couple of days. He spent a minute cropping them, so they looked like mug shots that he could flash to other witnesses if he needed to.

The website for African Goddess had little information, although he could tell it was a high-end place. The address was along the bougie retail stretch of Robertson. It was odd to find an African store in that neighborhood—like most cities, LA was heavily segregated, and Robertson was extremely white.

He shot Max a quick text:

At the office. Need anything?

Max could get any of their surveillance gear out of the safe himself, Slater knew, and he'd call if he actually needed help, but he'd been told long ago by a concerned shrink that emulating someone's social actions would build camaraderie, and Max had been doing things like this, talking to him for no practical reason. It made sense, if he really thought about it, that communicating would reinforce their collaboration, build up the vibe for this shared endeavor.

His reply soon came:

Caffeine, but I have that here. Did you know the Baltimore has two entrances but only one set of elevators? Guess where I am?

That meant Max had been on his feet all day in a hotel lobby, waiting for his philanderers, trying not to look like a stalker. Slater texted back:

Courage, mon ami.

Hefting the garments and their gossamer coverings over his shoulder, he rode down to the street and walked across to his car, where he laid them flat on the backseat. The streets were slow with lunchtime traffic, but then any attempted journey after eleven involved congestion. The twentieth-century fantasy of the freedom granted by the automobile was quashed by the sheer number of them; in those terms, Los Angeles was a failed experiment. Still, Slater couldn't imagine living anywhere else. Like Doris, he'd probably be here until they planted him.

Parking at a meter half a block up from African Goddess, he pulled the clothes out of the backseat and walked back along the swanky street of narrow little boutiques with hardly anything in them. It was a world apart from where he bought his clothes, downtown in a Latin-focused discount department store where the racks overflowed and half the clothes were on the floor.

In front of one of the little shops was a camellia, planted in a box and in riotous red bloom. It was the wild kind, gorgeous and gnarly and ungroomed, with lots of spurs, not the delicate cultivated varietal that looked like a bonsai rosebush. This one was even more dramatic in contrast with the chic minimalism of the boutique it fronted.

He assessed African Goddess as he approached. On display in the windows was ordinary women's wear, and as he stepped inside, nothing looked specifically African, although both staffers, a man and a woman, dressed in purple and gray and talking to a customer, looked like they had African roots. The guy looked at Slater as he entered, giving him a sour pointed once-over.

Slater held up the bundle of jackets and affected a Spanish accent. "For Mr. Pierre?"

"Take those in the back," he hissed, scowling and jabbing his thumb toward a curtained doorway.

That has to be Mr. Pierre, Slater thought, grinning to himself and ducking through the curtain. Carolina's assessment rang true—he seemed fussy. He hung the jackets on a clothes rack and looked around. There were a few other garments hanging there, and some shelves, a file cabinet, a lone desk with a computer. He wiggled the mouse, but the screen demanded a password. Riffling through the paperwork on the desk revealed only mundane invoices and bills.

Mr. Pierre came through the curtain, and speaking with a vaguely French accent, demanded, "What are you doing in here?"

"You told me to come in," Slater said.

"If you think I'm going to sign for those, it's not going to happen. I have to go through them first. You can wait, but not inside the store."

Mr. Pierre was older than he looked from a distance, and superficially kind of hot. Perfectly bald, he wore some kind of makeup over his whole head, giving it a satiny sheen, and a sleek gray vest over his purple shirt, with a little string tie that had a polished amethyst at the collar.

"Quality control issues?" Slater asked. "I'm surprised. Your merch looks a little"—he paused for effect—"cheap."

It had the desired effect, a flash of anger contorting Mr. Pierre's face. He glanced pointedly at Slater's shirt.

"Like you'd know anything about quality," he snarled, his accent forgotten.

"You brought some garments back to Kawada a couple of weeks ago, right after lunch. Remember that?"

A subtle chime sounded—the front door.

Mr. Pierre sighed in frustration. "Give me a second," he said, and pulled the curtain aside, stepping into the shop.

Slater stepped closer to the doorway so he could watch as Mr. Pierre approached the customer.

"Can I help you?" Mr. Pierre said, his accent thick and his tone impatient, as if she were an annoyance, maybe even a trespasser. The woman looked like everyone else in the neighborhood, far from being a vagrant. Slater couldn't hear what she said, but Mr. Pierre's answer was firm: "If you have any questions, Miss Odette will assist you."

When Mr. Pierre came back, Slater asked, "Why are you so harsh with your customers? It's almost like you want them to leave."

"You're no delivery boy," Mr. Pierre said, his eyes hard.

This guy was street smart, Slater could tell. He put his hands on his hips. "And you haven't always been a fancy Frenchman, have you."

Mr. Pierre scoffed. "I know you. I grew up with thugs like you."

Slater slapped him hard on one cheek, then quickly on the other, a powerful kovac.

Stepping back and touching his cheek, Mr. Pierre frowned, much less alarmed than a civilian would have been. "What was that for?"

"I am not a thug," Slater said intently, "but clearly we share an understanding of the world. Tell me about the day you went back to Kawada."

"Why would I tell you anything?"

Slater reached for his neck, and Mr. Pierre tried to dodge, but not quickly enough. Hand around his throat, Slater slammed him against the wall.

"Because if you don't, I'll choke you out with your stupid string tie."

His expression unfazed, Mr. Pierre gripped Slater's arm with both hands, but he didn't struggle. His voice distorted from the pressure, he said,

"It's called a bolo, and you should at least buy me dinner first."

Slater scoffed. This guy had been roughed up before, and knew better than to try to fight back.

"Sing, Mr. Pierre."

"You know, with one word I can get Miss Odette to call the cops. They'd be here in seconds."

"How would that look to those rich women out there browsing your *schmatta*?" Slater demanded. "Busting me would create a visually alarming dust-up—what your faux French compatriots would call a *rififi*. What would it do for your reputation to have photos of that online? You know how this works, Mr. Pierre. If you really wanted the cops here, you would have started screaming already."

Still calm, Mr. Pierre reverted to his French accent. "Please let go of my neck."

Slater obliged, dropping his hand, but stood close.

Mr. Pierre absently smoothed his collar. "So what if I brought product back to Kawada? They screwed up."

"I'm more interested in what you saw. Who was there? Was anything out of place?"

Mr. Pierre frowned. "I only saw Steve, and his workers."

"Are you sure? Think."

Pierre looked at Slater's chest. "There was

nothing out of the ordinary," he said finally. "Nothing that stuck in my mind, anyway. What happened there?"

"Something got stolen."

"And you think I did it."

"You weren't there at the right time."

"So you're investigating it," Mr. Pierre said, "even though you're not a cop."

"Correct."

"Well, it's nothing to do with me. They know me—I'm a good customer. They do good work most of the time. I have no beef with them."

Watching him closely, Slater decided he believed him. "Who do you know there besides Steve?"

"Carolina, of course, but none of the floor staff."

"What about Steve's wife?"

"Does she work there? I've never met the woman."

"What about Steve and Carolina? What are they like?"

Mr. Pierre shrugged. "Civilians. Everything on the up-and-up. Steve's polite to a fault, but he's not a pushover. You don't miss a payment deadline without hearing about it. Carolina's no dummy, but I've never seen anything to imply she was the light-fingered type." He paused, meeting Slater's eye. "Although we both know anyone can be a thief, given the right opportunity."

Stepping back, Slater handed him his card. "Call me if you think of anything else."

Not looking at it, Mr. Pierre slipped it into his breast pocket, eyeing Slater. "What about that dinner?"

Slater raised his eyebrows. "That's pretty nervy—I'm impressed. You're not really a fancy lad, are you."

"Honey, if there's one thing I know, it's how to spot my own kind."

Slater nodded. "You've got my number."

As he turned to go, Mr. Pierre called after him. "You mentioned the way we treat the customers."

"I did," Slater said, turning back.

"In high-end retail," he began, "there are two ways to handle people. Some stores have friendly clerks that welcome you warmly, treat you like a peer, in the hope that you'll be more likely to buy something because of that positive connection. The other way is to make you feel like you're not quite good enough for the merchandise, in the hope that you'll spend in order to prove that you're worthy. Each method works with different kinds of customers, but you can't do it both ways in the same store."

"And you're type B."

Mr. Pierre grinned and made an elegant little bow from the neck.

"Later, Mr. Pierre," Slater said, and stepped toward the curtain.

"I appreciate French cuisine the most," he called after him.

Walking through the store, he exchanged a curious glance with Miss Odette, who was talking to the shopper Mr. Pierre had condescended to. He'll be disappointed when he finds out Slater's maximum restaurant splurge was to go to an Anglo vegan burger joint rather than a cheaper sidewalk *pupusería*. Why would he shell out for haute cuisine when sex was free elsewhere? But it felt good to know Mr. Pierre was into him. That's why he'd volunteered the inside story on his sales technique, aiming to build a connection.

Back on the street, he walked toward his car. This trip had been a dead end, but maybe he'd get a hookup out of it, or a date, if Mr. Pierre had his way. That guy would be far too fussy to eat with, but he'd be fun to sleep with. Fussy guys were exuberant in the sack, and he probably had a plush apartment. Fashion victims usually did.

Checking his phone as he climbed into the Thunderbird, he found a text from Max:

I need a hand on my window-shade case.

Slater phoned him, and when he answered, said, "What's up?"

"Basically, I can't be in two places at once,"

Max said. "Do you have any time today for surveillance?"

"I'll make time," Slater said.

"I'm in Vegas, at least four hours out, and I need eyes on my target."

"Jesus, man, how did you get up there?"

"I followed the wrong woman. I just figured that out. It means my target is still in LA, and I can't get there for a while."

"Was it an intentional misdirect?"

"I really want to lie to you and say yeah, she fooled me," Max said, "but it was my own mistake. How many black-and-burgundy Citroën 2CVs do you think there are cruising around Brentwood?"

"More than one, I'm guessing."

"Can you check whether she's home, and if she is, sit on the house until I get there?"

"Text me the address. I'll go now."

"Thanks, man," Max said, sounding relieved. "I really hope I haven't screwed this up. If the 2CV is there, the target is home. She's about thirty, long dark hair, Latina, likes to wear short skirts and big earrings. The client lives there too, but she's out of town. If she leaves, I need to know who she meets."

"Got it," Slater said. "I'll let you know when I have eyes on the house."

Pulling into the traffic, Slater headed up

toward Sunset Boulevard. It would take Max a while to text the address, with those pudgy fingers and driving on the freeway, but he could get started toward Brentwood.

Surveillance was incredibly boring, even with the gadgets he'd acquired from the Russians that automated a lot of it. The upside was that it was almost meditative, with few distractions, so it usually gave him a chance to think. Even if the target was home, tonight would be a breeze, as there was a clear time limit—whenever Max got back from Vegas.

He took Sunset all the way, an easy winding drive, and got Max's text with the address before he was in the neighborhood. Cruising past the house, which was sprawling even by Brentwood standards, he saw the 2CV parked in the driveway. Circling back, he parked down the block, on the opposite side, with a view of the car and the front of the house. An overhead photo on the map on his phone showed no alley out back, and there was a thick hedge around the yard—anyone coming or going would have to come via the street.

He reached into the backseat for his binoculars, focusing on the house. The front door didn't look used, which meant the residents went in a side door, likely on the driveway in front of the Citroën. Either way, he'd see the target if she left, and he'd definitely see any visitors.

After he'd settled in, keeping one eye on the house, he texted Max.

> The car is in the driveway. I'll update you if anything changes.

Pulling up his tracking app, he checked on Conrad's whereabouts. He was out in the Valley, but not at home, the weirdo. What was he up to? Zooming in on the dot on the map, he was in a drugstore. Freaking duplicitous backstabbing moron. Why would he be skulking around a pharmacy? Buying microwave popcorn and Fresca and condoms? They gave those away for free if you went to the right kind of bar once in a while—not a stupid cop bar, but one with guys. Who was he sleeping with, anyway? He had to be sleeping with someone. Probably someone a lot saner than Slater. Yeah, well, sanity's relative, Punch-face, and it's overrated. It was too infuriating to think about, and he killed the app.

On the Web he looked up customer reviews for African Goddess. Some reviewers said it was a snobby place, and that it was upscale, and lots of them conflated those two concepts. "The best jacket I've ever owned," said one, and another, "cutting-edge upscale trendiness." It made sense that if you told people they weren't good enough for the stuff, some of them would believe it was inherently superior.

There weren't any reviews for Kawada Couture, but that was logical—Steve wasn't a label himself but rather manufactured clothing for labels, so there wouldn't be any awareness of Kawada among consumers.

He put the phone away and stared at the empty suburban street, watching the odd vehicle roll by. That was a great car, the 2CV, so odd, so French, nothing like Mr. Pierre, despite his affectation. He felt sorry for some of these people, the owner of that vehicle, whoever she was, so mistrusted by their loved ones that they fell under the gaze of people like Max and Slater. It always came down to money. You sign a prenup, and promise to be sexually exclusive forever, and then human nature kicks in, and you're sleeping around. Wealthy people protected their assets and their status by not letting them get dissipated by unfaithful husbands and wives. He looked through the binoculars again. The car had been well restored, with no dents, smooth paint, new tires. Whatever the target was up to, whoever she was sleeping with, at least she had that sweet ride.

Setting down the binoculars, he thought about his own case. He couldn't see a connection between the missing necklace and Silvana Lee, but surely he could find out more about her. She wouldn't have given her real name when she was running a con, so there was no point in searching for her, but maybe he could get more from the only person who had interacted with her—Carolina.

There was a guy named Mason that Slater used sometimes, when he needed an innocent-looking mooky Anglo front man. The guy called himself a psychic, which was patently bullshit, but he wasn't a grifter—he actually believed it. More importantly, he had some useful psychological tools.

Scrolling through his contacts, he dialed, glad that Mason picked up.

"It's Slater," he said. "Do you have some time tomorrow morning? I want you to interview someone—under hypnosis."

"I can do that. Who are we interviewing?"

"We'll discuss that tomorrow," Slater said impatiently. "Come by my office around eleven."

"I didn't know you had an office."

"It's new," he said, and rattled off the address.

"That's in the Fashion District. Sweet."

"What do you charge for a hypnosis session?"

"Well," Mason said, "it never takes more than an hour or so. Maybe three hundred?"

"That's fine. See you then," he said, and ended the call before the guy could ask any more questions.

Now he just had to get the witness to agree to it. Things might go easier if she had less time to think it over. Kawada Couture would still be open, he saw, glancing at the clock. He dialed the office number and asked for Carolina.

"I have a couple of follow-up questions," he told her. "Can I swing by in the morning?"

"I guess so," Carolina said. "But I told you everything I know."

"It won't take long."

"I'll be here. So did you talk to Mr. Pierre?"

"I did—he's quite a handful."

"Did he know anything about … the incident?"

"I don't think so," Slater said. "I'll see you tomorrow."

Slater set down the phone, his gaze focused on the inert 2CV up the street. Hopefully the psychic knew what he was doing.

——◆——

The car didn't budge, and no one came or went as darkness fell. Someone was home, it appeared, as lights came on inside the house, glowing yellow through the curtains. His stomach was grumbling by the time Max's matte-gray Challenger rolled up. Max spotted him and continued down the block, Slater watching in the rearview mirror as he pulled a U-turn and parked behind him, then got out. He was still wearing that ugly brown suit. Did he ever clean the damn thing? After Max stretched and rolled his shoulders, he climbed in Slater's passenger side, slumping into the seat and rubbing his eyes.

"I hate that drive."

"You hit traffic, if you left Vegas when we talked," Slater said.

"There's always traffic," Max said glumly. "So the target hasn't budged?"

"No one has come or gone. I don't even know if she's in there."

Max peered down the street. "The Citroën is there, so she's there. She only takes ride-shares when it's late and she's going drinking. I'm thinking with the wife out of town, she'll be stepping out tonight."

"So who is she sleeping with?"

"A guy, if you can believe that," he said, closing his eyes and leaning back onto the headrest. "The wife is not happy. She's the one who hired me."

Slater sighed. "Straight people are crazy."

"You said it, brother," Max said, but then held up a finger. "Wait—I'm straight."

"After five hours on the 15, I'd probably lose track of that too."

Leaving Max to watch the inscrutable house, Slater drove home, glad he'd been able to bite his tongue and not call him a dumb-ass, or berate him for tailing the wrong car to another state, just because he couldn't be bothered to write down a tag number. As annoying as it was to censor himself, not saying all that would make it easier to work with him; Slater knew that. Still, this whole human-relationships thing was a lot of freaking work.

There was a taco stand near his place that he knew could make them without meat, and he stopped to pick some up. He wanted to eat in the car, but knew he'd make a mess, so he held off until he'd parked in the garage and gone upstairs. Once he was inside he ripped open the bag and ate over the sink.

Sated, he stretched out on the sofa, content in knowing that there was a bottle in the cupboard waiting for him, the most patient and loyal lover a man could ever have, so predictable, so reliable. Insidious too, if Conrad's strident whining held any credence.

Pulling his phone out of his pants, he swiped through some faces and torsos on a hookup app, but none of them were especially arousing, and he'd just had someone here last night. Maybe Mr. Pierre would call, but he doubted it. Because he was interested in Slater, he'd be playing the long game: he'd act like he wasn't interested, waiting a few days, maybe a week, and then call, pretending he'd found Slater's card when he was taking his eight-hundred-dollar shirt to the dry cleaner. No guys tonight, he decided. Bourbon and sasquatch it would be.

In the kitchen he filled a tumbler and dropped an ice cube into it, then brought it back to the sofa, along with the bottle. He started an episode of the podcast and took a deep drink, reveling in the rich intensity of it, then setting the tumbler on the carpet beside his phone, shifting to get comfortable, following the narrator deep into the forest, sinking into oblivion.

———

It was cold when he woke up, huddled under the covers, in his own bed, he saw, his clothes nearby, strewn on the floor. Forcing himself to abandon the warmth of his bed, he went into the kitchen, where an empty bourbon bottle sat in the middle of the floor, one side of it crushed in. How had that gotten there? He stared at it for a minute, trying to remember. At least it wasn't made of glass—he'd be cleaning up shards for half the morning.

It really was morning, he saw, checking his phone, and he was going to have to hustle to meet the psychic. After he splashed cold water on his face, he picked a favorite from among his clean shirts—thank you, Rosa—and pulled on his jeans.

The Fashion District was a short drive across the 110 and through downtown. When he pulled into the surface lot across from his building, he checked the time. It was almost eleven. No Max, he saw, once he was in the office, but that was no surprise; he'd be sleeping off that nonsensical road trip. Slater had just dropped his satchel on his desk when he heard a knock on the door.

Of course he won't just walk in like a normal person, Slater thought, and went out to the front office to pull open the door for him.

"Hey, man," Mason said, stepping inside. "How great that you got your own space."

Mason was a tall redhead, way too pasty for

this climate but built thick, and borderline fuckable, despite being dressed like a bank teller, in chinos and a collared shirt, a dorky backpack over one shoulder and a bicycle strap forgotten around his right pant leg. He was exclusive with someone, Slater knew, but at least it was a guy, so there was always the glimmer of potential.

"Do you know it's exactly eleven o'clock, to the second?" Slater demanded. "You are so freaking Anglo."

"You seem annoyed. Most people appreciate punctuality."

Slater scoffed. "Come on in."

Once they were in his office, Slater pulled out his wad of cash and peeled off three hundreds. Normally he'd never do that, but Mason wasn't the kind of guy who would bail because he'd been paid in advance.

"Thanks," Mason said, grinning and pocketing the bills, then dropping into the chair in front of Slater's desk. "So what are we doing today?"

"It's all about information," Slater said, leaning back in his chair. "There's a witness in a case I'm working. If you hypnotize her, you can pull out more details about a given event, correct?"

"That's how it works. I've had good success with the technique. It's about accessing memories in the subconscious mind, so it's not actually psychic, per se."

"That's why it works," Slater said flatly. "And do not tell the witness that you're a psychic."

Mason shrugged. "It's your dime. What events are we asking her about, specifically?"

Slater briefly described the theft of the necklace, and Silvana Lee's grift. Mason pulled a yellow notepad out of his backpack and jotted down notes.

"I get the picture," Mason said finally. "I'll put her under and guide her to that moment, and then you can ask questions." He eyed Slater. "But you have to use your inside voice—no yelling, and no intensity. Just calm and cool, no matter what she says."

"I'm sure I can handle that," Slater said, scowling. "So where did you learn to do this?"

"At the library, mostly. There are a lot of books about it."

Slater's eyes narrowed. "How many times have you done it?"

Mason hesitated. "Including this time, twice."

"Fuck me," Slater snapped.

Mason held up his palms. "It doesn't mean I'm not good at it."

"If you're wasting my time, I swear I'll flatten you."

"Dude, chill. I know what I'm doing. If I don't get anything from her, I'll refund your C-notes. How about that?"

Slater watched him for a moment. "Fine," he said, and rose. "I have to go get her."

"Where is she?"

"Right down the block. I'll be back in a couple of minutes." Glancing around the office, he added, "There's nothing to steal."

Mason frowned. "Right, like that's the first thing I thought of."

"I know you won't try to jack me," Slater said, hands on his hips. "You're not that guy. If you did, I'd just go ask at the Episcopal church who confessed to stealing staples and printer paper."

"Episcopalians don't do confession," Mason said.

Slater scoffed and walked out.

"How did you know my people were Episcopalians?" Mason called after him.

Riding down in the elevator, Slater wondered if the guy was too obtuse to be all that fuckable. But that red hair was still tempting. He wanted to smell it, at least, all sweaty from cycling, even though it's not that warm out. Bury his face in it, even, and feel that milky skin. Other priorities, he told himself, striding into Kawada Couture's building.

Carolina was standing at one end of a cutting table, palms on the tabletop, head down, studying two piles of paper. She was wearing trousers today, cut to accent her curves. She looked up and smiled when she saw him.

"I wondered when you'd show up."

"No Steve today?" Slater asked.

"He'll be back soon. You need him too?"

"Just you. Would you mind coming to my office? I'm right up the block."

Carolina glanced at her paperwork, but then met his eye. "I guess. Will I need my coat?"

"It's beautiful out."

She shuffled her paper together and said something in Spanish to the guy at the other end of the table, who looked up from the fabric he was cutting. Slater caught only *Ibáñez,* and *Steve,* and *oficina.*

She led Slater to the elevator, and once they were out on the street, her stilettos clacked loudly on the pavement as they walked.

"Why your office?" she asked.

"I work with a professional interviewer," Slater said, "and my office has walls, so you won't be talking to the entire staff. Have you ever been hypnotized before?"

She looked at him sidelong. "Are you kidding me?"

"It's a technique we use to get at deeper memories. I figured there might be something from that day still buried in there that your conscious mind forgot."

"So you hired a hypnotist?"

"He's an experienced professional, and he induces a very light trance," Slater said confidently. "It's harmless."

"I guess I'm willing to try it." She grinned. "Just don't ask me anything embarrassing."

Slater eyed her, not sure if she was flirting with him. "It'll be strictly professional."

He led her into the lobby, past the day laborers.

"One of my vendors is in this building," Carolina said, "but I haven't been inside."

"It's not quite as nice as yours."

As they entered Slater's office, Mason rose and put his phone away. Slater introduced them and then went to Max's office to pull in a third chair. He shoved his desk toward the wall to make more room, and the three of them sat facing each other in the space in front of it.

"The way it works is that I'll talk you into an altered state of mind," Mason said, holding Carolina's gaze. "Then Slater will ask you some questions about the incidents."

"Incidents, plural?" she asked, looking to Slater.

"I'm still not convinced the necklace and Silvana Lee aren't connected," Slater said. "Even if they're not, maybe your subconscious will come up with something useful, so we can find her."

Carolina nodded. "I'd love it if you could."

"Can we dim the lights?" Mason asked.

"There's no window, so it's either like this or

pitch black," Slater said.

"I guess this will work," he said, and to Carolina, more gently, "Are you nervous?"

She crossed her legs and sat back in the chair. "A little, sure."

"The key thing to remember is that I can't make you say or do anything when you're under that your conscious mind wouldn't say or do."

"OK," she said, furrowing her brow. "Are you licensed? How long have you been doing this?"

"There's no licensing system in California," Mason said, gesturing widely, "but I took a series of courses and got a certificate about eight years ago, and since then I've perfected the technique. People want to be hypnotized for a lot of different reasons—to help them stop smoking, lose weight, and sometimes to find things they've lost, like, 'Where did I put Grandma's ring?'" He paused, his expression relaxed and amiable. "Not everyone can be hypnotized, but I'm up around ninety percent positive these days. If you're at all worried, I can assure you it's completely safe and has no lingering effects. Most people can even remember everything they said when they're under. Shall we try it?"

That's why he hired this guy, Slater thought, watching him talk. The wide-eyed earnest snow job, not a whiff of insincerity or subterfuge. He actually believed he was that skilled, so lying about it was justified, the means to an end—putting her at ease about how safe it was, priming her to go into the altered state. Most important, Carolina looked convinced, flicking her hair back and grinning confidently.

"Let's get comfortable in that chair," Mason said, "and when you're ready, close your eyes. Pay attention to your breathing. Slow and steady. Inhale … exhale."

He paused for a while, and Slater found himself thinking about his own breathing, how his chest felt moving rhythmically in his shirt.

Eventually Mason continued, his tone soft. "When you need to get out of town, where do you go—the beach, the mountains, or the desert?"

"I like the beach," Carolina said, her eyes still closed, "but not to relax. I went camping up at Kings Canyon last summer. Have you been up there? That place is really beautiful. It felt like an escape."

Slater frowned. Carolina didn't seem like the camping type—more like the type who'd be debilitated when a heel broke two minutes past the end of the pavement.

"That's great," Mason said. "Visualize that place, the forest up there. The sun is shining. You're walking on a trail, alongside a stream. You can hear the water running over the rocks, and the buzzing of insects, and the birds. There's a little wind high up in the trees, and it's making the pine needles sigh. It's calm, and the sun feels warm. It's really beautiful here."

Carolina sat, eyes closed, impassive, and Slater watched Mason, listened to his soothing voice, not sure if he was falling into the trance along with her or if he was just sleepy, last night's libation not yet completely burned out of his system. But he kept his eyes open, listening to Mason direct her deeper into the forest.

After he'd talked for a while, describing the landscape in more detail, Mason said, "Everything is really vivid now. Can you see that?"

"Yes," Carolina mumbled.

"You can see the leaves on the trees, each blade of grass. Isn't it wonderful how sharp and clear everything is?"

"It's wonderful," she agreed.

She was under, Slater realized.

Mason picked up his notepad and glanced at his notes. "Steve and Lillian are going to the opera, and Lillian came by the factory to try on that dress. You know the one. Look at that necklace she's wearing. Can you see how sparkly it is?"

"Yes," Carolina said. "Diamonds. I don't know what the center stones are."

Mason caught Slater's eye, and nodded to Carolina.

Trying to emulate Mason's calm, even tone, Slater said, "Lillian takes off the necklace and puts it on the table. Can you see that?"

After a long pause, Carolina said, "She's behind me. I'm working on my computer."

Slater thought about how Steve and Lillian had described the incident. "Lillian went into the changing booth. Can you hear her pulling the curtain around?"

Again a pause. "Yes," Carolina said, her voice strained.

"What do you see?" Slater said gently.

"Three outstanding checks," she said slowly. "What is wrong with these people? Don't they like money? All you have to do is drop it at the bank. You can even deposit it through your phone. Overlooking one check, I could understand, but three? Did their office burn down? Maybe their mail person is a kleptomaniac, but only steals the envelopes from me."

Slater glanced at Mason, who rolled his fingers, miming *Move it along.*

"You look away from your computer," Slater said.

"Because Lillian is screaming," Carolina said, her voice rising. "Who took what? What are you so upset about, woman? Take it down a notch."

"Remember the trail you're on?" Mason said. "The trees sighing overhead, the sun shining."

"Mm," Carolina managed, but she sounded uncomfortable.

"You feel so calm, so relaxed. Nothing could mess with this feeling," Mason said, looking at his pad. "No one can change the way you feel right now, not even Silvana Lee."

Carolina groaned.

"She comes into the office. What is she wearing?"

"Vermilion. That has to be wool. I don't know the designer. … Maybe it's bespoke. Accountants must really make bank."

She paused, and Mason waited patiently, glancing at his notes, then watching her.

"That skirt is so short," Carolina continued. "She must have a pelvic exam later. No way did she have those boobs when she finished high school. Even the hair. Is that real? The color certainly isn't. Of course you'd put the Clytemnestra over it, not under it, because it means you're money, that's the message here. Who puts a knot in a Clytemnestra? … So much foundation. She must buy it at the hardware store. … Those eyes," she said, her voice rising. "Do you really think anyone is fooled by those? I know your eyes aren't really blue. Who does that unless they're in a horror movie?"

"You're not looking in her eyes anymore," Mason said quickly. "She speaks to you."

Mason was making more notes, Slater noticed. That was so smart. He really was good at this, despite his lack of experience.

"Uh huh," Carolina said, and paused. "He was here in November. It seems a little early for a tax run through. … OK … Yeah, I can do that."

She was having a conversation with Silvana Lee, Slater realized. "What do her hands look like?"

"Vermilion. The nails match the suit. How does she type with those claws?"

"What about the shoes?"

"Stiletto pumps. Black. I'd totally wear those."

Mason looked at him and tapped his wrist. He wasn't wearing a watch, but Slater knew what he meant. Slater flashed his palms—*Do what you have to do.*

"Carolina, you're going to come back," Mason said. "As slowly as you need to, come back to Slater's office. You're going to feel good when you wake up."

They waited, and Carolina didn't speak, didn't move.

"Are you back?" Mason asked finally.

"Maybe," she said.

"Take your time, and when you're ready, open your eyes."

Carolina blinked and looked at Slater, then Mason. "Did it work?"

"Do you remember anything?" Mason asked.

"You were talking about Kings Canyon," she said, slurring her words.

"You look groggy," Slater said. "Are you sure you're all right?"

Carolina blinked distractedly. "I'm fine."

Slater looked at Mason, eyes narrowing.

"Sometimes it takes a minute to fully return to this plane," Mason said quickly. "Take it easy."

"You used a word to describe Silvana Lee," Slater said, looking back to Carolina.

Mason looked at his notes. "Clytemnestra?"

"That's the one. What does it mean?"

"It's a high-end clothing brand," Carolina said. "All they make is scarves, and they cost, like, twelve hundred bucks."

"Was Silvana Lee wearing a scarf?" Slater asked.

Carolina stared at him. "She was. I remember. Did I tell you that?"

Slater nodded. "You did."

"I guess I remember that too." She rubbed her forehead. "I feel like I've taken a sleeping pill."

"When you talked about the day the necklace was stolen," Slater said, "you remembered Lillian was screaming. You didn't seem happy with her. How well do you know her?"

Carolina shrugged. "I've only met her a few times. She doesn't come around the office, except once in a while to do fittings. I know she causes Steve plenty of grief."

"Do you think she's capable of pulling an insurance scam?"

"Honestly, I don't know," she said, concern in her eyes. "I hope not. Is that what you think?"

"I have to consider all the possibilities. What about Steve?"

She shook her head slowly. "No way. He's the salt of the earth."

"That's what he said about you."

"I should get back to work," she said, rising from the chair. Unsteady, she put her hand on Slater's desk.

Slater stood up, glaring at Mason.

"You'll be fine in an hour or so," Mason said. "Have an espresso. And maybe don't drive for a while."

"I take the metro anyway," she said.

"I'm going to walk you back," Slater said, and to Mason, "Can you copy me on your notes?"

Mason nodded, looking relieved. "I will."

Slater tucked his satchel under his desk and locked up the office. The three of them rode down together, and Slater told Carolina, "Take my arm."

As they stepped off the elevator, she looped her hand behind his elbow, and as they walked, he could feel her using him for balance. Mason said good-bye and stopped at a bicycle double-locked to a parking sign. Slater admired his butt as he stooped to unlock it.

"So did you learn anything useful?" Carolina asked as they walked.

"Maybe," Slater said. "Thanks for indulging me. I'm a little concerned that you're still groggy."

"It feels like waking up on Sunday morning. You know how it happens leisurely when you don't jump out of bed right away? I'm definitely getting more lucid."

"Think of it as a new life experience. Now you know what it's like to be hypnotized."

She chuckled. "The best part is that I can tell people I spent the morning in a windowless room being interrogated by two handsome men."

Slater grinned at that. It was interesting to see how people on the sidewalk looked at them—things were different when he had a glamorous woman on his arm. Passing glances weren't fearful or suspicious; it was more like they were pleased, or that they knew his role, his place, chatting agreeably with her. Paired with a woman, he was no longer an unknown, a potential threat.

SIX

By the time they got to her office, she had released his arm. Slater rode up to the factory with her. The place seemed busier, with more people around, several of them cutting fabric, the sewing machines humming, a guy boxing up wispy-thin orange dresses.

Steve rose from his desk, amiable but with curiosity burning in his eyes at seeing Slater come in with Carolina.

"The man from Cudahy Mutual," Steve said. "How is your research going?"

"Slater's office is right up the street, in the Del Rio Building," Carolina said.

"I know it well. That's where you did your interview?"

"It's easier to talk there," Slater said. "My

office has walls."

"Have you got any leads?"

"Silvana Lee was wearing a Clytemnestra scarf, which I didn't remember until today," Carolina said.

Steve's expression shifted, his brow furrowing. "Really? Which one?"

"That, I don't remember."

"What do you mean, 'which one?'" Slater said sharply, looking from her to Steve.

"He means the pattern," Carolina said. "There aren't that many of them, so they have nicknames: the fishes, the flowers, the bells."

Steve folded his arms and looked away, lost in thought.

"Wait," Carolina said, screwing her eyes shut. "It was the flowers. I remember. It's mostly pink. I can see it over the vermilion jacket. It's so weird to pull out that detail—I'm still halfway in that head space."

"Can you show me what it looks like?" Slater said.

Carolina stepped over to her desk, and Steve walked off into the factory. Slater stood behind her chair, peering over her shoulder as she typed.

"That's the flowers," she said, looking up at Slater.

"They're not flowers. They're blossoms," he said, staring at the image.

"That's different? How can you tell? It's so stylized."

"It's a cherry, or a plum. Probably a cherry. Look at those stubby little stamens."

Carolina gazed at the screen, then looked at him. "It's a drawing. Aren't you assuming a lot?"

"Definitely cherry," he said, standing erect. "I should go. Where's Steve?"

Carolina glanced around the busy factory. "Not here anymore, but I'm sure he'll be back. Do you need to talk to him?"

"Eventually," he said, and headed to the elevator.

It was odd that Steve had disappeared, he thought, riding down. Maybe it was the mention of the Clytemnestra scarf. If that meant something to him, why wouldn't he just say so? Maybe it was some vibe with him and Carolina, some straight thing. But he'd been looking for something like that, and hadn't detected any romantic affection, or secrecy, or jealousy. Still, there was something between them. Mutual respect, at the very least, or amity grown through a long friendship.

Rather than returning to his office, he crossed the street to his car and drove to the Financial District, pulling into the underground garage of the office tower that housed Cudahy Mutual. Handing his keys to the valet, he took the elevator to the thirty-ninth floor and walked into the lobby. The receptionist, in a dour blue blouse and a chignon, recognized him, he could tell, despite trying to mask her reaction.

"Is Della here?" he asked.

She frowned. "Will you let me warn her that you're coming? It's kind of my job."

"You don't need to cop an attitude with me," he said firmly, hands on his hips. "I'm not an unreasonable person." He gestured to her desk. "Go ahead, make your stupid phone call."

She picked up the receiver, still eyeing him. "Mr. Ibáñez to see you," she said into the phone, and then to Slater, "Go on back."

"I'm so glad I waited," Slater said intently. "It doesn't feel like you're wasting my time at all."

Della looked up from her desk when he strode in, and leaned back in her chair. "Hey, handsome. What have you got for me?"

"Just checking in," he said, and dropped into a chair. "There's something hinky going on at Kawada Couture—the place where your necklace was lifted—but I haven't figured out what it is yet."

"You talked to the claimant?"

"I interviewed her twice, and I don't believe anything she says. I talked to the husband too, and he was acting squirrely this morning, so I don't think I believe anything he says. One of the seamstresses who was there didn't see squat, and

I shadowed the office manager one night, but she claims she didn't see anything either."

"I get the picture," she said. "You think it was an inside job?"

"Maybe. I've built some rapport with the claimant's stepson."

Della shot him a weary look. "You're sleeping with him."

"Why would you think that?" he demanded. "I keep my dick out of my cases."

She held her hands up. "I don't need to know how you do your work."

"What do you know about Clytemnestra scarves?"

"Fancy," she said, raising her eyebrows. "Way out of my income bracket."

"You dress fancy," he said, assessing her billowy low-cut top.

"Not Clytemnestra fancy. I'm not paid well enough to drop a grand on a three-foot piece of silk."

"So not many people wear them."

"In some circles, I'm sure everyone wears one."

"Where do you buy them?" he asked.

"There's a shop on Rodeo Drive. It's the only one in town." She looked thoughtful. "Is it connected to the necklace?"

"Maybe. I want to track down a woman who was wearing one."

"People who can afford that kind of clothing could be pretty mobile. Even if she's an Angeleno, she could have bought it in New York or London or Shanghai."

"Good point," he said, and stood up. "I basically just wanted to tell you that I've got nothing to tell you."

Della grinned. "It sounds like you're making progress, at least. And don't terrorize my receptionist on the way out. She thinks you work for a drug cartel."

Slater scoffed. "That sounds a little racist. She must watch too much television. What's her name?"

"Crystal."

Walking through the lobby toward the elevators, he said, "Have a good afternoon, Crystal."

She frowned, suspicious. "OK."

Slater sighed. He'd tried. Some people just weren't very friendly.

Once he'd retrieved his car from the valet, he headed west, toward Rodeo Drive. If there was only one place to buy a Clytemnestra scarf, maybe someone there would remember a dramatic figure like Silvana Lee.

The short stretch of retail had several valet parking stands for its monied consumers, but the street felt quiet, even more than Robertson had. That was probably a corollary of it being more upscale, he realized, and since there was no street parking, he left his car with a valet and walked to the Clytemnestra shop. There were scarves on the mannequins in the window, but inside there seemed to be an underwater theme, with aquariums, fish, and kelp painted on the walls, integrated into the displays.

The shop looked abandoned, but he must have tripped a doorbell when he walked in, as a tall blond in a dark-blue suit came out of the back and stepped up to the counter.

"Hello there," he said, smiling broadly. "Are we shopping for a wife, girlfriend, fiancée?"

Slater hadn't anticipated that—in upscale places, looking the way he did, he half expected the bum's rush.

"We don't have any of those," Slater said, and seeing his nametag, added, "Brian."

"That sounds even more interesting."

Slater spread his arms, leaning on the edge of the counter. "Your sales model is the friendly method rather than the snobby way, I see."

"Are you in upscale retail?"

Brian was probably in his forties, and his hair looked blond all the way to the roots. Slater liked the hint of a challenge underlying his words, and who didn't like blonds?

"Do I look like I am?"

"You don't look like you're shopping for silk

scarves either," Brian said, his tone still breezy.

"So how many patterns does Clytemnestra have?"

"Seventeen active, and thirty-three retired."

"Do you sell a lot of the cherry blossoms?"

"Most people call it the flowers, but I know the one you mean. It's based on a medieval Japanese family crest. And yes, it's one of the most popular active patterns."

"Does the store keep track of its customers?" Slater asked. "There can't be that many of them."

"Of course," Brian said, his smile fading.

"I'm looking for a woman who wears the flowers."

"So you're a private dick," Brian said, raising an eyebrow.

"It depends who's asking," Slater said evenly. "Play your cards right, and you might just get your hands on it."

Brian laughed, covering his mouth like a boy. "You're not one for innuendo."

"Well, you're the one who pulled that word out of the 1920s."

"I know I don't have to tell you that type of information is confidential."

"That's why I brought my friend Andrew, from Tennessee," Slater said, and set a folded twenty on the counter.

Brian eyed it and looked back at Slater. "You

realize the merchandise here starts at eight hundred dollars? And that's for the seconds—the junk that's on clearance."

"Your clientele might be one-percenters, but I bet they don't pay you to be. Are you on commission?" Slater waved an arm at the empty store. "You don't seem to be doing a lot of trade."

"Very astute, sir. Very astute," Brian said.

"Maybe Andy's friend General Grant would help," he said, and set down a fifty.

"I don't know," Brian said, cocking his head.

"Not enough?"

He hesitated. "It's not that."

"If you don't want cash, what do you want? You were talking about dicks—I could smoke you."

Brian's eyebrows shot up. "I can't tell if you're being serious."

"Serious as an eight-hundred-dollar scarf," Slater said, and folded his arms. "I'm pretty good at it too."

"Oh, man," Brian said. "I bet you are."

"Is anyone else here? Let's go in the back."

He looked past Slater toward the street. "Deal."

Slater reached for the bills on the counter, but Brian covered them with his palm before he could get to them.

"I'll hang on to these boys, thank you," he

said. "You should have led with the hummer."

"Fine," Slater said, frowning. "But first we talk about your customers."

Brian waved to the other end of the counter, where a computer screen was perched. He walked over and peered at it as he typed.

"We get names and addresses when we do a card transaction, but lots of customers are cash only, so we keep notes."

"What kind of notes?"

"Their name, if they mention it. What designers they're wearing, age bracket, and incidental information that comes up in conversation, like their hometown, marital status, who recommended them to Clytemnestra."

"It sounds like a lot of note-taking," Slater said.

"Like you said, there aren't that many people to keep track of. Does your friend have a name?"

"Try Silvana Lee."

Below the counter the keyboard rattled. "Nothing," Brian said. "When did she visit us?"

"At least six weeks ago."

"What did she look like?" he asked, eying him.

"Middle-aged, Asian."

Brian grinned. "That's the majority of our clients. They love Clytemnestra. My theory is that they land at LAX and make this their first stop."

"I think she's local. Blond hair, wearing blue contacts."

Brian looked thoughtful. "I think I remember someone like that." To himself, he said, "What was her name?" After a minute of typing and peering at his screen, he said, "Here she is. Blue contacts. I wrote the name 'Ms. Lee' and 'no wedding ring.' What did you say her first name was?"

"Silvana," Slater said. It was hard to believe she had used that name twice. "Do you have a photo?"

Brian shook his head, typing. "There's not much in my notes. I wrote 'Asian, blue contacts, blond wig'—"

"You're sure it was a wig?"

"Have you met her?" Brian asked, meeting his eye. "Trust me—nobody has hair like that from nature. She must have mentioned that she lived in the Ampulosa Residences, or had us deliver something there, because I also wrote that down."

"Seriously?" Grinning, Slater pulled out his phone and thumb-typed a note with the name of the building. "Is that in LA?"

"I think it's a high-rise downtown," he said. "Anyway, that's all I have in my notes."

"Brian, you are a rock star."

"I feel a little corrupt, but that was an easy way to make seventy bucks."

Slater looked up at him. "Don't forget the second installment."

"I thought you might skip out on that, once you got what you wanted."

"A deal's a deal," Slater said sharply, and looked toward to the entrance, then back at Brian. "What?"

"I just can't believe you want to blow me."

"If you're not into it, you've still got the cash."

"No—I'm into it," he said. "Come on back."

Slater walked around the end of the counter and followed him into the stock room. There were subtle security cameras in the store, but he couldn't see any in here. Pulling on Brian's shoulder, he turned him around and kissed him, exploring his mouth. This guy knew what he was doing, knew how to connect, his mouth soft and yielding. Slater reached for his belt buckle, but Brian took his hand, stopping him.

"I can't get all sloppy and untucked. Someone might come in. But I can blow you, yeah?"

"When a man is tired of blow jobs, he's tired of life," Slater said.

"Whatever," Brian said, and pushed him back against a desk, unbuckling his belt.

Slater was already getting hard seeing this guy sink to the floor, carefully hiking up his pant legs before kneeling. He must do it a lot—he was really good at it, intuitive. Slater didn't even have to guide him. Beyond getting smoked, watching his head bobbing and meeting his eyes looking up at him was such a turn-on. What was it about blonds? He came, finally, grunting, and grabbed Brian's head to stop him.

Brian got to his feet, and Slater chuckled.

"What's so funny?"

"You have that face," Slater said.

"Hummer face?"

"That's a good name for it." Slater took a few breaths, recovering, then put his hand on Brian's neck. "Are you sure there's nothing I can do for you? I feel a little selfish."

"I got what I wanted," he said. "You could give me your phone number."

"Do you have something I could clean up with?"

"There might be a scarf around here somewhere," Brian said, walking to a cupboard and tossing him a roll of paper towel.

Slater buckled his belt and gave Brian his business card. Walking out to his car, he thought about how the guy had framed the transaction, as corrupt. It was far from that—Slater had paid him for a piece of information, and as long as he didn't tell his corporate masters about it, nobody got hurt. Except Silvana Lee, of course, but she had it coming.

People had such weird ideas about money, and what their jobs were worth, and propriety. Brian had been more willing to trade a blow job for information than cash, which was even more illogical, as it had less value. Sex was free, so paying for something with it was like paying with twigs and leaves. Either way, he wouldn't be itemizing any of it on his invoice to Della.

Once he had his car back from the valet, he parked on a side street a few blocks away and looked at his phone. Conrad was at work, the lazy idiot. And Brian was right—the Ampulosa Residences were downtown, near the stadium. He knew that area, bristling with bland newly built residential towers, the units owned by Chinese investors as a way to stash their capital abroad. Because the apartments sat empty, it made the neighborhood sterile—there was no demand for groceries, or restaurants, or bars, the only economic impact being the meager wages of a maid who came in and vacuumed up the dust once a month.

Driving downtown, as darkness fell, he turned on his headlights and let his phone guide him on surface streets, along a completely counterintuitive route, presumably avoiding some late-afternoon traffic. He parked up the block from the Ampulosa Residences and walked to it. Even in the dark he could tell there were no cameras on the outside of the building, and when he entered, there were none inside the lobby either.

A young guy with a Latin look sat alone

behind a small U-shaped counter. Not bad looking, Slater decided. The dark suit could be a plainclothes outfit, but he looked too soft to be security; this guy was a concierge. He rose as Slater approached.

"What unit is Ms. Lee in?" Slater asked.

"There are several people in the building with that name."

"Most of them are back home in Shanghai, though, right? She lives here. Snappy dresser, blond hair, wears blue contacts."

"I think I know who you mean. I can phone her."

"Or just tell me what unit she's in."

"I can't do that," the concierge said, shaking his head.

Slater palmed a twenty and set it on the counter between them.

"Are you kidding me?" he demanded.

"I've offended your morals," Slater said, "or it's not enough?"

The guy eyed him, then pocketed the bill, looking satisfied. "She's not home anyway."

"That wasn't the question."

"I really can't give out that information. I could get in trouble."

"What's your name, son?"

"Ben," he said, frowning.

"That ship has sailed, Ben," Slater said, and

slapped him hard, lightning fast, and again, a hard kovac.

"What the fuck, man?" Ben demanded, stepping back and bumping his chair, which rolled into the wall with a *clunk.*

"We've already established a fiduciary relationship. If you don't fulfill your part of it, I'll have no qualms about beating your ass."

"You touch me again, and I'll call the cops." His eyes darted to the phone below the counter.

"That's your prerogative," Slater said. "But ask yourself what would be less work—risking your tenant's wrath for giving me one little number, or explaining to your boss why you took my cash, and how you got a black eye and a broken arm at work? Do they provide your health insurance?"

Red from the kovac and flushed with adrenaline, Ben watched him, calculating, his face betraying that familiar mix of anger and fear. It was just a matter of time now, and possibly more fist work, Slater knew, until he made the right choice.

"I'd get away with it too," Slater said. "There are no cameras in here."

Ben's eyes went dead. He'd made his decision. "She's in 1560."

"Such a sensible guy. You have great skin too—I'm glad I don't have to mess it up." He set another twenty on the counter. "So why is that, no security cameras?"

"The building is advertised as discreet," Ben said, glancing at the bill and quickly pocketing it. "There are no cameras anywhere, and the parking spaces are enclosed, so nobody can see who's here."

It was probably aimed at corporate lotharios who wanted a hidden place to cheat on their spouses. Going unseen would be a lot easier in a neighborhood like this, empty and sterile most of the time, except during a stadium event, when the crowds of people streaming by wouldn't notice who was here anyway. That also made it a perfect hideout for a high-end con artist.

Someone came in the front entrance, and Ben said "Good evening," getting a mumbled acknowledgment. Slater didn't look, watching Ben and waiting until the elevator dinged and rumbled open.

"You see who's here, though," Slater said.

"Most people come in through the garage. They don't have to see me or anyone else."

"So you wouldn't have noticed Ms. Lee's car, or know the make?"

"No way," he said, shaking his head.

Slater grinned at him. "Good night, Ben."

Back on the street, he walked past the garage entrance, a dark ramp down to a firmly closed rolling shutter. That was part of the anonymity package: any vehicle entering would be out of view of the street while it paused for the shutter to roll up. There was no alley, but around the side of the building was a service bay, large enough to back a moving truck into. The wide door had a metal shutter over it, but there was also a regular-size fire door, unmarked but with a handle on it, and a standard deadbolt. That was his way in.

Walking back around toward his car, he glanced into the lobby at Ben, seated again and with his head down, bathed in the blue-white glow of a computer screen. Slater pulled out his phone and dialed Max.

"How's the love triangle?" Slater asked him when he picked up.

"I think I got what I need. I'm meeting the client tomorrow."

"Where are you now?"

"At the office, writing up my notes," Max said.

"Excellent. I need some help tonight. Have you had dinner? I'll bring you a burrito."

"I'll be here. Get me beef or chicken, not pork."

Slater climbed into the Thunderbird, driving a few blocks to a bougie gentrified fresh-Mex place with stupidly named tacos and burritos that cost three times what they would in his neighborhood. But it was right on the way, and the spice level wouldn't give an Anglo guy like Max an aneurysm. Inside he ordered two vegan burritos to go. Max would never know the difference.

When he got to the office, Max was absorbed in his computer. Slater set the bag of food on his desk.

"That smells great," Max said appreciatively.

Slater pulled the chair closer and handed Max a burrito.

Unwrapping it and taking a bite, his mouth half full, Max said, "So what are we doing tonight?"

"I'm going to show you how the Russians open doors."

SEVEN

After they'd eaten, and Slater had explained his plan, he went to open the safe, pulling out a bright yellow flash drive with an adapter cable dangling from it. His phone already had everything he needed loaded on it, but Max's didn't.

"Give me your phone," Slater said.

Standing behind him, Max looked unsure. "It's that Russian stuff, huh."

Slater had to admit he was wise to be dubious. Anything that couldn't be bought at a hardware store, the surreptitious gear, both the hardware and the software that he used for surveillance, came from a shady Russian tech vendor down a grimy back alley in Glendale. The apps could very well be spying on him—he'd be surprised if they weren't, as all the big legit tech companies and cell carriers were quite frank about the fact that they did that—but so far there had been no fall-out from it, and he paid the Russians enough for this stuff that he had the impression, at least, that he was buying their discretion.

"I can't say it's safe," Slater said. "I've never had a problem with it, although it's hard to figure out what it's telling you sometimes."

Max sighed and handed over his phone. Slater plugged in the flash drive, and it took a minute to remember how to do it, but eventually he found the app, "Lock Check," and installed it, Max leaning close to watch. When it was finished, he handed the phone back and tossed the flash drive into the safe.

"Can we do a practice run?" Max asked.

"Try it on the office door," Slater said, and pulled his satchel out from under his desk, extracting a length of cable with a thin metal probe at one end, the size of a key. He handed it to Max.

"How does it work?" Max asked, examining it.

"Plug it into your phone, then run the app I just installed."

Max peered at the bottom of his phone and plugged in the cable, then stepped out to the reception space and opened the front door. Their offices were behind the elevators, and no one ever walked back here unless they were lost. It was well after business hours anyway, and the hallway was deserted, the building quiet. Max tapped at his phone, and the screen went black, displaying a circle with the word "готов" inside it.

"What does that say?" Max asked, turning the screen toward Slater.

"I've no idea. Put the probe into the lock."

Max dropped to one knee and gently slid it in like a key. On his phone the circle turned red and displayed "ошибка."

"Red means it's not working. Pull it out a little," Slater said. "It's temperamental."

Max adjusted the probe, and the circle turned green, now reading "243."

"That's the key that'll fit," Slater said. "Sometimes it gives you more than one number, and you have to try them all, but just one makes it easy."

Slater went back into his office and pulled the key collection out of the safe, carrying it out to the reception desk. It was an industrial binder, made of heavy fabric that couldn't easily be cut, with loops for a padlock on the ends of the zipper. Slater never bothered to lock it, as it was kept in the safe. Zipping it open, he flipped through the heavy sheets that contained dozens of master keys in little plastic pouches. He hefted up the case and held it out for Max, who took the key from the sleeve labeled 243 and tried it in the lock. It turned easily, snapping out the deadbolt.

"Amazing," Max said, twisting it back.

"It doesn't always work," Slater said, "and it's only good for standard hardware-store stuff. With high-security locks, forget it."

"Most people don't have high-security locks," Max said, handing him the key.

Slater put it back in its sleeve and loaded the case into his satchel, then went to the safe, kneeling in front of it to get the other gear they'd need.

Looking up at Max, who was standing in his office doorway, he said, "You should leave your weapon."

"Good call," Max said.

They both knew there was a big difference between doing something illegal and doing something illegal with a firearm. Max took off his jacket, then his weapon, holster and all, and locked it in the safe.

"Want me to drive?" Max asked, as they walked across the street to the parking lot.

"Yeah—your car blends in better."

It was just a few blocks to the Ampulosa Residences, and Slater directed him to a side street to park.

"This neighborhood is so quiet," Max said, pulling up to the curb and killing the engine. "Isn't that weird? All these high-rises are apartments and condos."

"No one actually lives here," Slater said, pulling

out his phone. "I'm going to make a phone call, and you're going to do the talking."

"Why can't you?"

"Punch-face knows my voice." He told Max what to say, and spent a minute fiddling with his phone to route the call through his number-spoofing service. It was gratifying to actually be using it, considering how much he paid to have it available. Finally he handed the phone to Max.

When the concierge picked up, Max said, "Could you connect me to Ms. Lee? She's in 1560." He waited, phone to his ear, and then spoke again. "Thanks anyway. I guess I'll catch her at the office."

"Nice embellishment," Slater said, taking the phone back.

"There's no answer on the apartment's land-line."

"We're good to go, then." From his satchel he pulled out a blue ball cap and snapped it open, pulling it onto his head, and handed a matching one to Max.

"I thought you said there were no cameras in this place," Max said.

"There aren't, but there might be some on the neighboring buildings."

"Can I really wear a ball cap with the suit?"

"I am so taking you shopping," Slater muttered, eyeing his jacket.

Max chuckled and pulled on the cap, adjusting the bill low over his brow. Slater reached into his bag and produced two sets of black latex gloves.

As he pulled on his pair, Max said, "How long will we have inside?"

"Three or four minutes. More than that, and anyone who's missing their Wi-Fi or cell service will start to freak out."

They climbed out of the car, Slater slinging his satchel over his shoulder. It was heavy, with the key case and the other gear inside it, and he shifted it into the middle of his back. Walking to the building's delivery entrance, he kept his head down, scanning the street, but there was no one around to notice them.

Max didn't need any instruction, his phone already in hand, the cable attached, the new app running. Standing against the door with his back to the street to conceal his actions, he slid the probe into the lock. It quickly came up with the green circle and "193." Max dropped his phone in his jacket pocket, and Slater swung his bag onto the ground and flipped through the key case, not pulling it out of the satchel. Once he'd found 193 he stood, shifting the bag onto his back again, and slid the key into the lock, opening it easily with a satisfying *thunk*.

Max grinned and followed him inside, closing

the door. They were at the top of a stairwell. Slater scanned for cameras. Ben had been telling the truth—there was no surveillance in the building, not even here.

Max tapped the sign on the wall with a black-gloved finger:

EXIT LEVEL 1

DOWN TO LEVELS P1 TO P3

"We want to go up, not down," he said quietly.

"We'll go up from the parking garage," Slater said, and trotted down the stairs.

Pulling open the door into the garage, it didn't look at all like a public parking lot, but more like a storage facility, with closely spaced individual garages, each with a steel shutter. Some were open and empty, a few had cars parked in them with the door up, but many were closed.

"It's so sneaky," Max said quietly as they strode along the aisle. "You'd never be able to tell if your target was home. These people must be paranoid, or have ironclad prenups."

"I'm sure some of them are just basic crooks, like Silvana Lee."

Signs for the elevator pointed to the far end of the floor. A car was waiting, and with his latex-clad finger, Slater pressed the button labeled 15. As the doors closed, he pulled a pair of safety glasses out of his satchel, handing them to Max,

153

then took out his own pair. Pencil lights were mounted at either temple, like a jeweler's glasses with built-in loupes, but for a very different purpose.

"How do you turn it on?" Max asked, flipping them over and squinting.

"There's a switch on the left side, on the inner surface."

Slater donned his own pair, adjusting his cap to fit over them. The tiny lamps didn't cast light detectable by the human eye, but in the UV range, visible to cameras, they produced a glare bright enough to completely obscure their faces. They hadn't needed them in a building without security cameras, but Silvana Lee might have her own surveillance inside her apartment.

The elevator door opened on the fifteenth floor, and Slater scanned the abandoned hallway. On the door marked 1560 he knocked and listened, waiting before knocking louder, but heard no movement. He pulled his satchel around, flipping it open.

"Mark the time," he told Max, and then switched on the radio jamming device, a dull-gray metal box with a lone toggle switch and an indicator light. It lit up in brilliant blue—intended to make it hard to miss later if he forgot to turn it off.

"It's working—my phone just went offline,"

Max said. "May the neighbors forgive you."

It was an extreme tactic, jamming the cellular and Wi-Fi frequencies, even in a small radius, but it would effectively knock out most cameras, and even wireless alarm systems.

"Go," Slater said, setting his satchel on the carpet and pulling open the key case.

Max fiddled with the probe, his pudgy latex-clad fingers looking sweaty and inept. His phone displayed the red "ошибка" message. Slater took a breath and waited, resisting the urge to grab the thing and take over. Max gently manipulated the probe, and a single number appeared in the green circle.

"Yes," Max hissed, and tucked his phone away.

Slater quickly found the key, twisting it in the lock and pushing into the apartment. The lights were off, but in the indirect illumination of the metropolis that was diffusing in the balcony doors, everything looked white, beige, and tan—the walls, the carpet, and in the kitchen, right in front of them and separated from the living room by an open counter, all the appliances. Slater stood listening for a second while Max closed the door and started scanning the room.

"No alarm panel," Max said quietly.

"Check for cameras," Slater said, clicking on the lights and stepping into the living room, where two short sofas faced a coffee table. It looked like the generic stuff people rented for real estate staging, or hotel furniture. Beyond the living room on the balcony sat two dusty disused outdoor chairs.

The kitchen was spotless, unused, the fridge empty. There was just one bedroom, and Slater stepped in and clicked on the light. The bed was made, and on the dresser stood a Styrofoam model of a human head. A wig stand—Brian was right again.

The floor of the closet was littered with women's high heels and a single pair of men's dress shoes. They were huge, like skis, stylish and gaudy in that idiosyncratic Eurotrash way. From the rail above hung jackets, skirts, and colorful blouses, along with a man's suit and two dress shirts, much larger than the other clothes. The suit was made of iridescent gray fabric, way too flashy for a guy with a regular office job.

Slater took out a hanger with a petite red jacket on it, wishing he could feel the fabric without his latex glove. Pulling it open revealed a short skirt hanging underneath. He'd seen this outfit before, in a grainy black-and-white video. True vermilion. This was definitely Silvana Lee's place—and it looked like she had a boyfriend.

Closing the closet again, he carefully pulled open the drawers in the dresser. Most of the contents were women's clothing in small sizes, but one drawer had big T-shirts, guy socks, and tighty-whities.

There wasn't time to dig any deeper, but he stepped into the bathroom and flicked on the light. Cosmetics containers littered the surface around the sink, along with two toothbrushes. On the floor was a wicker wastebasket, and he dug through the balled-up tissues and wads of cotton, finding only product packaging and other trash. At the bottom, though, was something more interesting—a little scrap of light cardstock, one corner caught in the weave of the wicker. "LAS to LAX," it read, in bold lettering, and below that, "S. Lee," with a date, three months ago. A boarding pass stub. Silvana had been to Vegas.

Slater pulled out his phone and photographed it on the carpet, then put it back under the other refuse, positioning the basket where he'd found it. Three months seemed like a long time not to empty the trash, but maybe it had been overlooked, caught at the bottom.

Back in the front room, he found Max looking in the kitchen cupboards.

"No cameras, and the kitchen trash is empty," he said. "Where do you want to put your camera?"

"In here—that one should have a view of the front door." Slater gestured to the electric socket on the back wall, above the countertop.

"Are you sure? It's almost at eye level."

"Nobody uses this kitchen. It'll be fine." He scrabbled in his satchel for the cameras, sealed inside a plastic zip-top bag. There were four of them, two beige and two white, two ovoid and two square, to blend in with the most common wall-socket designs. He pulled out the square white one. It had three metal prongs, like an electric plug, mounted on a very thin plate whose face was painted to mimic the three holes of the wall socket. At a glance or from a distance, it blended in, and looked like a regular unused socket, but within the largest black-painted shape was a pinhole that contained the camera lens.

Slater pushed the device into the socket, making sure it was flush. It looked pretty blatant to him, but most people wouldn't even notice it, at least until they tried to plug something in. Even then, hopefully they would assume it was a child-proof cap rather than a spy camera.

There was no way to tell whether it was working, as the device had to connect to the cell network, and that wouldn't happen with the Russian radio jammer running. They'd been here long enough as it was.

"Let's go," Slater said quietly, and Max opened the door to the hall, doing a quick scan before stepping out. Slater followed, easing it closed and using his master key to lock the deadbolt.

"Time?" Slater asked, following Max toward

the elevator. He reached into his bag and switched off the radio jammer.

"Four and half minutes," Max said, glancing at his phone.

Once they were in the elevator, they pulled off their eyewear, and Slater switched off the UV lights, stuffing them in his satchel. The elevator made it to the parking level without stopping, and they headed silently back between the rows of private stalls to the fire stairs, then up and out to the street.

Once they were beyond the service bay and on the sidewalk, Max said, "Success?"

"It's definitely Silvana Lee's apartment. Did it seem off to you?"

"It was way too clean," Max said. "Like a hotel room after housekeeping has been through."

"More than that," Slater said, peeling off the latex gloves. "There was no TV, no desk, no computer. No stack of mail, or bills, or take-out menus."

"Maybe she's just fastidiously tidy, and takes her laptop with her."

"Maybe. It kind of feels like she doesn't live there. Like you said, it's like a hotel. The bathroom was lived-in, but not the kitchen. Her clothes were in the bedroom, and some guy's stuff—shirts and shoes and a suit."

Max pulled off his ball cap and dropped his

sweaty crumpled gloves into it. "A boyfriend? Or maybe she dresses masculine sometimes."

"They weren't hers—the sizes were much bigger. I'm thinking she uses the place to hook up with a guy."

As they climbed into Max's Challenger, Slater glanced around at the empty street, but they weren't being observed. As Max drove, Slater checked on the wall-socket camera. The message that the app gave him, "связанный," was inscrutable, but it was definitely connected—half the screen was a fuzzy low-light image of Silvana Lee's kitchen.

"The camera's working," he said.

"Right on," Max said, slapping the steering wheel. "Can you see the front door?"

"Just the top foot or so, but it's in the frame. It'll definitely trigger a motion alert when someone opens it."

"Do you want me to drop you at the office, or at your car?" Max asked, turning onto their street.

"I need to go upstairs. Don't you need your weapon?"

"Not before tomorrow morning."

"What time are you meeting your client?"

"After lunch," he said, pulling up to the curb in front of the Del Rio Building.

"So at ten, I want to see you here. We're going suit shopping."

Max laughed, but Slater paused before climbing out.

"I'm not messing around," he said sharply.

"If you think it's that important, I'll be here," Max said.

"Thanks for your help tonight."

"It's part of the deal," he said, and waved as Slater closed the door.

Upstairs, Slater moved the gear from his satchel into the safe, glad to be free of the heavy key case. He took a quick look around, then went down to his car.

The more he thought about it, driving home, the more he knew something wasn't right with Silvana Lee. The only halfway normal thing in that apartment was the bathroom sink, with all the cosmetics. Everything else felt staged.

Waiting at a red light, he thought he should probably try to find a hookup, even though the adrenaline rush of crashing Silvana's apartment left him feeling exhausted. He'd sort of had sex with Brian at the scarf store today; maybe that was enough. Yeah, he decided, it counted. He could take the night off.

On the way home he stopped at a liquor store and bought three fifths of bourbon, which the clerk loaded into a bulky paper bag. Glancing at the security monitor while he waited, it took a second to realize he was looking at himself—he'd forgotten he was still wearing the blue ball cap.

At home he hung the cap on the back of the door and set the bag on the kitchen counter, pulling out a bottle, pouring a tumbler full, and slamming it. He had to gasp afterward as his throat burned. He poured another and put an ice cube in it, then sat on the sofa to pull off his boots. Stretching out, he put an arm over his eyes, too tired even to fire up *Sasquatch Search*, instead listening to the roar in his own mind.

EIGHT

aking in bed, naked and achy, he lay there for a while, catching up to reality. Silvana Lee's apartment, he remembered. Max was such a good sport, going along with it so wholeheartedly, not once whimpering in fear. Max needed a new suit, he remembered, and forced himself out from under the warm covers into the cold air.

There was nothing substantial in the fridge, of course, but he ate a pickle, staring absently at the paper bag from the liquor store on the counter as he munched, and then a mouthful of salsa from the little takeout container. It wasn't very spicy, but it wasn't meant to be an entrée either. There was a granola bar in the cupboard, and he ate that and made a cup of cowboy coffee before he got dressed.

When he walked into the office, Max had the safe open and was strapping on his holster.

"Reunited," Slater said.

"I feel naked without it," Max said, and pulled on his jacket, the same freaking ugly one he wore every single day.

"Time for new clothes," Slater said. "Let's go."

"Want me to drive?"

"We're walking," Slater said, and led him out to the elevator.

A block away they went into a fluorescent-lit men's suit store, one of dozens in the neighborhood, racks of garments stretching far into the back. The clerk, a woman dressed in jeans and a plain white blouse, approached them. She said something genial to Slater in Spanish.

"We're looking for a couple of suits for my friend here," Slater said.

She looked to Max, speaking with a Spanish accent. "Do you know your size?"

"No idea."

"Let me get my tape," she said, and walked away.

Max leaned toward Slater. "This stuff is kind of flashy, don't you think?" he said quietly.

"Of course it is. It's where the Norteño musicians get their outfits." Slater pointed to the wall of fame behind the register, where several rows of photos, autographed in thick black ink, depicted entertainers in sharp suits and cowboy hats, beaming and posing with their musical instruments.

Gazing at them, Max looked concerned, but dutifully pulled off his jacket when the clerk came back. She measured around his chest, and the length of his arms.

"Are you going to wear the suit with or without your holster?" she asked.

"I always wear it."

She nodded, unfazed. "We'll leave a little room."

"How about one of these?" Slater said, flicking through a rack of jackets with a metallic pattern, reflective squares separated by a grid of black fabric.

"I can't wear that," Max said, his voice rising.

"We have it in gray instead of the mirrors," the clerk said.

Slater nodded. "Let's see it."

"I'll look insane," Max said as she walked off.

"Insanely stylish," Slater said, meeting his eye.

The clerk handed Max a jacket, similar but more subdued than the mirrored one. "This should be your size."

Max pulled it on, and looked in the mirror.

"It fits," the clerk said. "You can wear the matching pants, or just plain black."

"Really?" Max said, turning sideways and

looking dubiously at his reflection.

"We'll take it," Slater said.

"Don't I get a say in what I'm going to be wearing?" Max demanded.

"No," Slater said firmly. "You've demonstrated no aptitude in that area." To the clerk, he said, "This needs a navy-blue tie."

She nodded and went to find one.

"All I need now is a red ball on my nose and a fright wig," Max said.

"You're looking too closely. From a distance, it's cool."

The clerk held a tie up to his neck. "It's a good combination," she said.

"Sold," Slater said. "We also need a suit in charcoal gray."

"That sounds more my speed," Max said, pulling off the grid-pattern jacket.

"Gray is for weddings, funerals, and babysitting only," Slater said firmly, and called to the clerk, "We'll need one in seersucker, and one in red too."

"Red?" Max exclaimed.

The clerk cocked her head, looking at him. "Maybe dark red."

"Show us what you've got," Slater told her.

She soon reappeared with a blue-and-white summer seersucker as well as a dark red jacket, which she handed to Max.

"I can't pull this off," he said, stepping back to the mirror and slipping it on.

"Of course you can," Slater said. "You'll wear it to meet-ups when you want to intimidate someone. The message is that you're dangerous."

"Or unhinged," Max said.

Slater strolled farther into the store and found a midnight-blue paisley suit. "This one too," he called to the clerk, and she found the right size for Max to try on.

"It's perfect for night work," Slater said. "You could walk into any bar in the city and own the place."

"You think?" Max said, looking at himself in the mirror.

"This one needs a dark-red tie," Slater told the clerk.

Eventually Max tried on all the pants, and the clerk marked them for hemming.

"I'm not sure I need five new suits," Max said, assessing the collection.

"No more brown," Slater said sharply. "I'm sick of looking at it."

Max looked to the clerk. "Is he right, or am I?"

She gestured widely. "You look good in all of them."

"You would say that—you're selling them."

"Listen to your friend. Gay guys are good at this."

"How did you know he's gay?" Max said.

She grinned. "When I ask customers to undress, they always flirt, like you did, unless they're a priest, or with their wives, or gay."

Max frowned. "You get priests in here?"

Slater pulled out his wad of cash and told her, "Ring me up."

"Wait—why are you paying?" Max said.

"It's my contribution to our collaboration. You're going to look sharp, and that benefits me too."

"It kind of makes me feel like a gigolo, or a kept man," Max said.

"That only applies if you're putting out," Slater said. "This is just business."

"What about for you?" the clerk asked Slater, looking up from the register. "You could wear the modern cuts. You have the body for it."

"I don't wear suits," he said, and peeled off the bills.

She made a quick phone call, and by the time Slater had his change, a cheerful young guy had appeared.

"This is the tailor," she explained. "He works a few doors down. He'll do the cuffs while you wait."

This guy, he'd definitely flirt with, Slater thought, eyeing him. He felt his phone buzz in his pocket, and stepped away from the register, standing beside a mannequin wearing a dark-green jacket with black-and-white key-board lapels. Jeff Kawada was calling him, he saw, looking at the screen. If he just wanted more sex, Slater didn't need to talk to him—but the guy was involved in Slater's case.

He picked up, answering "Ibáñez."

"Have you seen my dad today?" Jeff asked.

"Not since yesterday," Slater said. "What's going on?"

"He and Lillian are both gone, and the house is messed up. I don't know what happened. I—I didn't know who to call."

"Messed up how?"

"Tossed, like a burglary," Jeff said.

"When did you last see them?"

"I don't know," he said, his voice rising. "Sometime yesterday?"

"Are you at the house now?"

"I am."

"Sit tight," Slater said. "I'll be right there. Don't move anything."

Ending the call, he went back to the register, where Max was chatting with the clerk. The tailor and the suits were gone.

"I have to go," Slater said. "Work."

Max nodded. "Which suit should I wear to meet my client?"

"I'm not your dad," Slater said irritably.

"You just picked out my clothes, and paid for

them. You're more dad-like than my actual dad."

"OK," Slater said, and ran a hand through his hair. "You're giving her bad news, right? Has she paid you yet?"

"Not the full amount."

"There's your answer—the red."

Slater walked down the block to his car, waving at the parking attendant. They never asked to see his pass, probably because the Thunderbird was so recognizable. Once he was on the street, he phoned Steve, but it went to voice mail without even ringing—his phone was switched off. Should he try Lillian? No, he'd talk to Jeff first. He dialed Kawada Couture's number, and Carolina answered the phone.

"It's Slater—has Steve been in today?"

"He left a message on the office line at seven this morning, before anybody was here," Carolina said. "He said he wasn't coming in, and I was in charge today."

"Does he do that a lot?"

"Never. Should I be worried about him? Do you know where he is?"

"I'm going to try to find out," Slater said, and ended the call.

Cruising west to Hancock Park, he pulled the Thunderbird to the curb in front of the Kawada house, then walked up the immaculate lawn and pounded on the door.

Jeff pulled it open, looking rattled. "Dad's still not answering his phone."

His concern seemed authentic, Slater decided, and followed him into the front room.

"I told you not to clean up," Slater said, looking around.

"Not here—the bedroom was tossed."

"Show me," Slater demanded, and Jeff led him upstairs.

"This is the master," Jeff said, walking into a big room.

Slater's entire apartment would fit inside it. The bed was made, and it was mostly tidy, but the big walk-in closet, the size of Slater's bedroom, had been ripped apart—clothes on the floor, women's shoes strewn around, paperwork dumped and scattered at the far end. Something made of porcelain had been smashed, the detritus on the carpet and above that a dusty white scratch where it had struck the wall. Slater spent a minute looking carefully at the mess. It seemed to be more on Lillian's side, with Steve's hanging clothes untouched, only a couple of his drawers pulled open.

"Someone was in a hurry," Slater said, stepping back into the bedroom. "You have no idea who did this?"

"I wasn't here," Jeff said, standing far from the closet. "I thought they were in bed when I got home last night. I didn't even look for them until this morning when they didn't come down for breakfast."

"What time did you get home?"

"Eleven thirty, maybe."

"Have you talked to anyone else? Their friends, or relatives?"

"I called Carolina," Jeff said. "Dad left her a message that he wouldn't be in the office today."

Slater nodded, hands on his hips. So far Jeff's story tallied with what he already knew.

"It's so not like him," Jeff continued. "Do you think they could be kidnapped—or worse? Should I call the cops?"

"Don't do that," Slater said. "He wouldn't have left a message for Carolina if he was kidnapped. Looking at the mess, I'd say this was a search, not an abduction."

"How can you tell?"

"For one thing, there's no blood."

Jeff looked toward the closet again, his brow furrowing.

"Did either one of them have anything valuable in here?"

He shrugged. "I don't know. Lillian has a lot of jewelry, but I don't know if she keeps it here."

Slater went back into the closet, treading on the clothes and opening the drawers on Lillian's side. Some of them were already open and empty, their contents presumably on the floor now, but there was no jewelry. Either she kept it elsewhere, or someone had taken it. He crouched to examine some of the scattered paperwork. There were receipts for shoes and clothes, a credit card statement, a bill from a medical insurer, all with Lillian's name on them. Standing up again, he looked around for a minute, thinking through what might have led to this.

"Why did you call me?" Slater asked, stepping back into the bedroom.

Jeff gestured helplessly. "You seem like the kind of guy who'd know what to do."

Slater eyed him for a moment. He believed him, he decided.

"What about their vehicles?" he asked.

"I checked," Jeff said. "Both their cars are gone."

"So they're probably not together. It's Friday—do they ever go on spontaneous weekend trips?"

"Dad wouldn't do that without saying so—he'd tell Carolina, at least, if not me. I know Lillian goes away sometimes, but I don't know anything about that."

"Where do they go if they do travel?" Slater asked.

"I've never heard of them taking any kind of trip," he said, flapping his arms. "Dad's always here or at the office, and who knows what Lillian does all day."

"Think, Jeff," Slater insisted. "No beach house, a condo at a ski resort, a pied-à-terre in New York for fashion-industry work?"

"He does have a ranch, but it's far. We used to go when I was a kid. I haven't been there in years—since he got together with Lillian."

"Give me the address."

"It's way out in the desert, in New Mexico, so it doesn't have one. But I can show you on a map."

Jeff headed toward the door, and Slater took a last glance at the closet. Someone had been looking for something. He wondered whether they'd found it.

This had to be Jeff's bedroom, Slater thought, following him down the hall. It had a small bed with a baseball-print duvet, and great corner windows with a view of the street, a desk positioned in front of them.

"Somebody likes heavy metal," Slater said, assessing the band posters on the wall.

"When I was sixteen," Jeff said, grinning and sitting at his desk.

"No one took over your childhood bedroom?"

"I don't think Dad wanted me to leave, or grow up, or come out."

Jeff turned to his laptop, lifting it open and

spending a minute tapping at it, finally pulling up a map.

"There," he said.

Slater leaned in to look. "It really is in the middle of nowhere."

"He loved that about it."

"Text me that. So what's it like? Is there a house?"

"Ranch house, barns, and lots of open space. It's civilized, though—there's electricity and Internet."

"Who's there when he's not?"

"He rents the land to a local, and pays someone to grade the road and check on the plumbing, but no one lives there."

"Do you know any of those people, or how to contact them?"

Jeff thought for a moment. "I don't. I knew one of the neighbors as Uncle Tom, but I don't even know his last name, or where he lives."

"OK," Slater said, digesting it all. "What about downtown—do you know where he parks at the factory?"

Jeff frowned. "One of those surface lots, right around the corner."

"What does he drive?"

"A silver Lexus."

"Do you know the tag?"

"The plate number? How would I know that?"

But his expression changed. "Do they put it on the registration card?"

Slater gestured impatiently. "Yes, they do."

"Dad makes me keep a copy on my phone, in case it ever gets towed. He says you need it to get the car back."

"Show me."

Jeff pulled out his phone and found the document, handing it to Slater.

Slater tapped at the screen and sent it to himself, then handed the phone back. "Do you have one for Lillian's car?"

Jeff pulled it up, again handing it to Slater. "Are you going to look for them?"

"Are you sure this is right?" Slater asked, frowning at the screen. "This card is for a Ford."

"She drives a little red Mustang."

"Lillian? She seems more like the Mercedes type."

Jeff shrugged. "I told you, she's damaged. Maybe it's her midlife-crisis car."

"I'll let you know what I find out," Slater said, sending the document to himself and handing the phone back.

"You're leaving?" Jeff said, rising from his chair. "So what am I supposed to do?"

"Do what you'd usually be doing. Didn't you say you're supposed to be writing?"

"What if whoever tore up that closet comes

back? Maybe I should hang out at your place."

"Do you remember what my apartment is like?" Slater demanded. "That's the last place you want to be. Nobody got hurt here, and nobody's coming back here. Text me the minute you hear from either one of them."

"What are you going to do?"

"Find them—or find Steve, at least—and figure out what's going on."

Jeff frowned. "How?"

"Don't ask me that. It's what I do, and I'm good at it."

"So confident," Jeff said, and then his expression softened. "It's part of what makes you attractive."

Slater scoffed and headed toward the door. "Ciao, scion."

"One more thing," Jeff called after him.

"What?" he demanded, turning back.

Jeff hesitated. "You know, I never had sex in my high school bed."

Slater put his hands on his hips. "I wish I had time. Maybe after all this is over."

"Dude, we're both right here." He waved at the bed.

"I've got stuff to do," Slater said irritably.

"Just a kiss good-bye, then."

Slater sighed, and stepped over to him, cradling Jeff's face in his palms, leaning in and tasting his eager mouth. He slid his fingers into Jeff's hair, his cock swelling in his jeans. Jeff's arms encircled his waist. The guy was right, they were already here. It wouldn't take that long.

Pulling away, he asked Jeff, "Have you got a condom?"

"Yeah," Jeff said, grinning, and went to get it.

When he came back, Jeff was unbuttoning his shirt. Slater pulled him onto the bed, sliding his hands into his pants, squeezing his stiff cock and probing inside him, then stripping Jeff's pants off, and unbuckling his own belt.

"You're going to fuck me with your clothes on?" Jeff asked.

"I said I was in a hurry."

"It's actually kind of hot," Jeff said, and ripped open the condom, rolling it on for Slater.

Slater was soon inside him, starting slowly but eventually pounding him, one arm wrapped around his neck. Such a beautiful guy, so responsive to being touched. Nose buried in the back of his neck, Slater came, groaning with the intensity.

Pulling off the condom, he stepped off the bed and dropped to his knees, then pulled Jeff to the side of the bed, taking his cock into his mouth. It was surprising how hard he was—one of the perks of being young. Jeff moaned and ran Slater's hair between his fingers, his fist clenching as he came.

Slater climbed onto the bed with him and flopped onto his back, arm under Jeff's neck, catching his breath. Before long he stood up.

"Love me and leave me?" Jeff said, folding his hands behind his head, contentment in his gaze.

"I was about to walk out of here," Slater said, tightening his belt. "That kiss was a total bait-and-switch."

"I wasn't sure if it would work, but I'm glad it did."

"Well, now you can say you've updated your high-school bed."

NINE

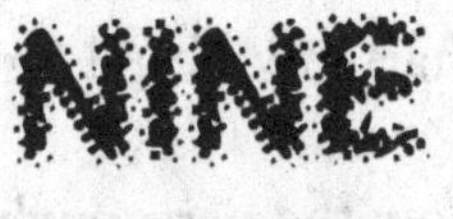

The guy was fun, but not boyfriend material, Slater thought, walking out to his car. Sexy and sweet and book-smart, but too innocuous. Slater needed to be with people who understood his world, his stratum, the dank underbelly down beneath the civilized realm. A guy like Jeff would try to drag him out of it.

Speaking of trash, he thought, Conrad had better be at work. Climbing into the Thunderbird, he pulled up the tracking app on his phone, relieved to find him at his station. Slater dialed his cell.

"What do you need?" Conrad answered.

"That's not the only reason I call you."

"Yeah, it is."

"I was just wondering—how are you feeling

today? Emotionally, I mean? How is your soul?"

"Cut the bullshit, or I'm hanging up."

"Fine," Slater said. "You guys have those license plate readers. Can you check if there were any hits today on a specific tag?"

"No freaking way," Conrad said, his tone hushed. "I don't have access to that."

"You're a smart guy. You'll figure out a way to get into it."

"I barely know the person who could check."

"So be friendly," Slater said. "I know you can be sociable. You're social enough with Doris."

Conrad's tone changed. "Aw, Doris. She's so sweet."

"She actually said that she finds you abrasive, and she wishes you'd stop bugging her."

"Are you sure that's not what she said about you? She worries about you, you know."

"As is her prerogative. You're not allowed to," Slater said. "Not anymore."

"I can't help it, Slater. You're like a crème brûlée—all scorched and crusty on top, but kind of a sweet mess once you break through that."

"Better a crème brûlée than total fucking betrayal," Slater said, raising his voice.

Conrad was silent for a second, then said, "Text me your tag. I'll see what I can find."

"There are two, actually," Slater said quickly. "I need whatever you can find as soon as possible."

"Yes, sir—would you like a lemon slice with that?"

Slater hung up on him, then found the registration documents on his phone and texted the plate numbers.

Crème brûlée, he thought, pulling away from the curb and scoffing. Such a moron, labeling him, judging him, conspiring against him. He didn't even want to think about what he'd told Doris, or vice versa. It was too infuriating, and he pushed it out of his mind as he drove downtown.

Leaving his car in the lot across from his building, he walked to Kawada Couture. When he stepped off the elevator, he spotted Carolina standing at a table with one of the workers, speaking Spanish, discussing the oddly shaped pieces of manila card arrayed in front of them. Patterns for garments, he realized.

She looked up at him, and her expression shifted. It wasn't fear or alarm; he knew what those looked like. Maybe Slater showing up here reminded her that something was wrong.

"Any news?" she asked, stepping toward him.

"I wanted to ask you the same thing."

She folded her arms. "Nothing since that phone call."

"Can I hear it?" he asked, and Carolina walked over to her desk, picked up the receiver, and punched in some numbers. She listened for a second, then handed it to him.

"It's Steve," the recording said, and it was definitely his voice. "I'm not coming in today, so you'll have to hold down the fort." His tone was businesslike, with no suggestion that he was under duress. After he spoke there were a few seconds of dead air. Wherever he'd called from was noisy—outdoors, near traffic.

"Can you tell what number it came from?" Slater asked, handing the receiver back to her.

"His cell," she said. "I checked."

"When did you see him last?"

"With you," she said adamantly. "After I got back from our hypnosis session, he seemed kind of distracted. After that, he was just gone—no explanation."

"Do they travel, him and Lillian?"

"Not without planning ahead, and he would have told me." Her eyes narrowed. "Wait—is she gone too?"

"I'm not sure. I haven't talked to her. Have you?"

She flicked her hand dismissively. "I don't even have her number."

"So you have no idea where Steve would go," Slater said, "or what he'd be doing?"

"None. Do you think we need to be worried?"

"He left you that message, so I'd say no."

From her expression, he could tell that his

words hadn't done anything to allay her concerns.

"Call me if you hear from him," Slater said, and headed to the elevator.

On the walk back to his office, his phone rang. Conrad, he saw when he pulled it out of his jeans.

"The Ford plate came up nada," Conrad said, "but surprisingly the Lexus got a hit. Seven hours ago it was parked in the underground lot at Union Station."

"That's when it entered the lot?"

"No—patrol drives around inside from time to time with a plate reader. It could have been there for a while, even a few days."

"Excellent," Slater said. "I owe you one."

"Take a night off, then. That's my payback."

"What are you talking about?"

"You know what I mean," Conrad said.

"It's not like you ever wanted me to abstain when we were together. We had a lot of fun, you and me."

"You're drinking when you're alone, Slater. I know you are. It's not a good tangent."

Slater couldn't go off on him, not after he'd just done him a favor. Instead he dug for the "polite words," a shrink had once called them, when she'd been trying to show him how to use them. "I hear what you're saying."

"Can we talk about it, at least?" Conrad said.

"Not at this time," he said evenly, breathing

hard, then, breezily, "Love you; mean it." He ended the call. Fucking moron—it's none of his damn business. Not anymore.

Nobody would leave their car at Union Station unless they were catching a train. Steve could have gone anywhere. Instead of going to his office, Slater crossed to the parking lot to retrieve the Thunderbird. He needed to look at Steve's car.

Even though the station was just a few minutes' drive, it took him a while to find the parking lot, driving around the front, then the back. Eventually he asked someone walking out of the employee lot, who directed him to the bus plaza, and sure enough, that's where the entrance to the underground garage was, half hidden between the bus ramps.

Pulling up the registration card that he'd taken from Jeff on his phone, he cruised around slowly, and spotted several silver Lexuses, finally finding the one with the right plate number on the third level down. He double-checked the tag, then pulled into a space farther along the row. Killing the engine, he reached into the backseat and grabbed a pair of black latex gloves from the box he kept there, pulling them on and then climbing out, walking toward the Lexus.

Glancing around to make sure he wasn't being observed, he pulled on the door handle, but Steve's car was locked. He put his hands to the side window to peer in, but apart from a lone tissue box on the backseat, there was nothing in view, nothing out of place.

In his own car again he peeled off the gloves and pulled out his phone, but there was no cell signal, so he drove up into the daylight and parked on a nearby street, in front of a diner. It made him feel leery, as the central jail was right around the corner, and this place was always crawling with cops. He dialed Jeff, who picked up right away.

"Hey, man—any news?"

"When you went to the ranch as a kid, did you drive?" Slater asked.

"Usually. We also took the train sometimes—Dad loves trains."

"Loves them how?"

"Looking at them, riding them. He'd drive one if they'd let him. I remember tramping around rail yards on vacations. When we went to Japan, my mom wanted to see temples, and he wanted to ride the bullet train."

"You got off near the ranch?"

"I don't remember the name of the station," Jeff said. "It was a small town. We'd rent a car and drive an hour or so. Do you think he's out there?"

"I've no idea. I'm just narrowing down the possibilities. We'll talk soon," he said, and ended the call before he could ask him anything else.

Jeff had texted him the location of the ranch. He pulled it up on a map, then zoomed out to see what cities were nearby, and then searched for passenger rail lines. It was still possible to get out there by train—stations in Gallup and Albuquerque were on a direct route from LA, and both were within a couple of hours' drive of the ranch. The schedule showed an overnight train every day, leaving here in the early evening.

He set his phone in his lap, looking out at the quiet street. That torn-up closet had definitely been searched, but what he hadn't told Jeff was that it also looked like there'd been a low-stakes scuffle. Logically it would have been between Steve and Lillian. It was sheer stupidity to get in the middle of a boy-girl fight, but both cars were gone—they weren't together now. Even though he had an inkling of where Steve was, it would be more interesting to find Lillian.

Picking up his phone, he dialed her number, but it went straight to voice mail. She'd turned off her phone too. He looked up the Kensington Club, and called the number.

"I'd like to speak to Lillian Kawada," he said, when the receptionist answered.

"One moment," she said, and when she returned a minute later, "Are you sure she was coming in today? She's not on the list for any classes, and she's not at the pool."

"Thanks anyway," Slater said, and hung up.

So there was nothing on Lillian, and only a tenuous lead on Steve. It was a huge gamble to go out to that ranch—it was way farther than Vegas, and he'd thought Max was pretty stupid for going up there on a poor assumption. He watched a deputy in uniform cross the street in front of him, on her way to the diner.

A glimmer of how it all fit together was coalescing in his mind. He needed to talk to both of them. The more he thought about it, the more it felt like Steve had gone to the ranch. When Conrad had dumped him, Slater had worked hard to fuck a lot of guys, the way he had before they'd gotten together. It was a way to reestablish an earlier pre-Conrad reality. Maybe the ranch was like that for Steve.

Twisting the key in the ignition, he pulled away from the curb and headed back to his office. When he went in, Max was behind his desk, wearing the dark-red jacket with a blue necktie. The other new suits were hanging on his office door.

"You look freaking fantastic," Slater said. "If you weren't packing heat, I'd shove my dick in your face right now."

"I'm glad I'm strapped, then," Max said. His eyes narrowed. "You're kind of raunchy sometimes."

"It's just my way of saying that you look sharp."

"Would you say that if I were a woman?"

"Of course I would," Slater said, hands on his hips. "But if you were, that suit would have to be cut differently."

"So you're an equal opportunity pervert."

"Did you get paid?"

Max grinned. "I did. She was pissed about the wife's nocturnal activities, but she paid up, and in cash. The photos were irrefutable."

Slater nodded. "Photos always sell it."

"She also said, 'I love that suit.'"

"From a lesbian, there is no higher praise," he said, and Max laughed.

"So I'm taking a road trip," Slater said.

"The necklace?" Max said, his brow furrowing. "Where to?"

"New Mexico."

"Wow—I hope that's a solid lead."

"Can you keep an eye on Silvana Lee? The camera will ping if she or the boyfriend show up at her pad."

"Sure," Max said. "You want me to tail her if she trips the camera?"

"I just want to know if she's around. I'm going into the desert, so I'm not sure how long I'll be in cell range—can we install the camera software on your phone?"

"Let's do it," he said, heaving himself up out of his chair.

Max followed him into his office, where Slater opened the safe and handed him the bright-yellow flash drive and its adapter cable.

"It's the one that starts with 'p-o-3,'" Slater said.

Max connected the drive and scrolled slowly through the list of software, some named in legible Roman letters with English words and some in Cyrillic, nodding when he found "розетка." Once he had it installed, he opened the app, which revealed a grainy black-and-white image of Silvana Lee's kitchen counter and the top of her front door.

"Looks like it's working," Max said.

Slater leaned in to look at the screen. "You'll get a notification if the camera detects motion within that frame."

"I hope I don't get searched, what with all this illegal software. It's pretty incriminating."

"I should have told you—there's a fix for that," Slater said, winding the cable around the flash drive and tossing it into the safe. "When you go to unlock your phone, instead of your code, type 112112. It wipes all the surveillance stuff. Anyone watching you will just think you flubbed the code and had to enter it again."

Max repeated the sequence. "That's easy enough to remember. I wonder why those numbers?"

"Ask the Russians," Slater said flatly. "Anyway, if you're under duress, you have a way to erase the software before you unlock it."

"It's ingenious."

"Thanks for doing this," Slater said, meeting his eye. "I'll let you know when I'm back in town."

"You're leaving now?"

"Tonight," Slater said. "I need to get some sleep first."

———◆———

When he got home, he poured himself half a tumbler of bourbon, just enough to take the edge off, he told himself, and slammed it. It was still midafternoon, but he knew how to sleep anytime, anywhere. He'd learned to do it on jobs when there'd been lots of waiting around. Once he'd even slept on a concrete slab with no padding except his own clothes. The key, he'd found, was to position his body symmetrically, every bone balanced left and right. Sleeping now, despite the daylight, in his own bed, would be a comparative cakewalk.

Stripping off his clothes, he shut the bedroom door to make it darker and set his alarm for nine p.m. Leaving then, he'd miss traffic, and if he was right about the drive time, he'd get to Steve's ranch sometime in the morning.

It felt like no time had passed when he woke

to his phone beeping insistently at him, but he knew it had; it was dark out. After he showered and dressed, he stuffed some clean clothes into his satchel, then got on the freeway a few blocks from home. He didn't bother with navigation, as he wouldn't need it until he was past Phoenix, and the 10 went all the way there from right in his own neighborhood. Going via Phoenix was a little farther, but the northern route through Flagstaff might get snow in February, and his tires weren't made for that.

Once he was past downtown and cruising through the endless Inland Empire, he phoned Jeff.

"Where are you?" Slater asked him.

"Home. No one's been here, and Dad's phone is still off. Have you found anything yet?"

"Not yet. Does Steve have guns?"

"God, no—why?"

"What about at the ranch? Are there long guns?"

"He's totally pro-gun control, Slater. He wouldn't even know how to use one."

"What happened to Steve's first wife? I assume that was your mother."

"She died when I was in high school. Why does that matter?"

"I need a broader picture," Slater said. "Is Steve the kind of guy who'd have a mistress?"

"No way. He's a straight arrow, and extremely loyal. To a fault, considering he's with Lillian."

Driving up the San Gorgonio Pass, rain started splattering on his windshield, big drops streaming through the beams of his headlights. It wouldn't last long, he knew. Ahead of him lay twelve hundred miles of desert.

———·———

It felt odd to listen to *Sasquatch Search* with a clear head. There was more detail, or maybe he was retaining more of it, with nothing to look at in the darkness but the broken white line and truck tail lights. No way could he do that himself, set off into the woods in search of the elusive creature; Slater was a city guy. But Carolina had talked about Kings Canyon, hiking in the woods up there, and she was pretty urban. Maybe he could handle it too.

He made a couple of stops for gas, the latrine, and food to eat in the car, and he was two hours past Phoenix, heading east on back roads, up over the mountains, before the sun finally appeared. Killing the podcast, he pulled on his sunglasses to face the glare of dawn. Once the sun was up and out of his eyes, the landscape was dramatic—myriad shades of red and pink rock and vibrant green foliage. This was their time to flourish, all these desert dwellers, during the winter rains, before the long dry months when their color faded to the more familiar muted dark green.

Just before he got onto an even smaller highway, he pulled into a gas station in a crossroads town. Despite the bright sun, it was bitterly cold when he climbed out. Why hadn't he brought a jacket? He'd thought of snow tires, why not clothes?

After he'd fueled the Thunderbird, perusing the racks of snacks before he asked for his change, Slater glanced up, catching the eye of a bearded guy with a heavy work coat and a red trucker's cap, walking toward the exit. Even central casting couldn't have produced such an authentic redneck look. The guy held his gaze for a second, and as he turned away, muttered "wetback."

Slater went to the till and set down his apple, and a bag of almonds, and some puffy bags of highly salted snacks.

The guy behind the till, who looked Latin and was probably still a teenager, said, "I hear stuff like that all the time too."

But Slater wasn't paying attention to him, instead looking through the doors, watching red-hat stroll out to his pickup, dusty and ratty and with those stupid oversize tires. It was the only vehicle here besides his own—no witnesses.

He strode outside, approaching the guy from behind, catching his driver's door before he could pull it closed, and thrust it wide open. Red-hat bellowed in surprise. Grabbing the lapels of his coat, Slater heaved the guy out of the truck. He scrabbled for the steering wheel, but it was too late—Slater had the momentum, swinging a boot in front of his legs and throwing him over his shin onto the gritty pavement. The guy was big, but slow, and as he rolled over, Slater was ready with a quick punch to the nose, then another.

"Why do you make me do this?" Slater shouted at him, deftly stepping out of range of his meaty grasping hands.

The guy looked dazed, unprepared for this, blood trickling from his nose into his mustache. He tried to sit up.

"Why do you make me hurt you?" Slater screamed, kicking him under the chin.

Red-hat's head snapped back, his hat tumbling to the pavement, and he slumped flat. Slater kicked him in the kidney, but it was like striking a sack of potatoes—there was no reaction. He watched him for a second, then stooped to feel his neck. The guy's heart was still pounding. He hadn't expected him to lose consciousness— big mouth, weak constitution. Sliding a hand under his head, stifling the instinct to recoil at the sensation of his unctuous hair, Slater felt for damage, but the skin was smooth, and the occipital bone intact. There wasn't even any blood.

When he stood up, the kid from inside appeared beside him.

"Did you kill him?" he asked cheerfully.

"He's out cold, but he'll be fine," Slater said.

"You forgot your snacks." The kid handed him a plastic bag.

"I didn't pay you," Slater said, still watching the redneck.

"The change from your gas will cover it. You should go."

Slater looked at him, and looked around at the eaves of the building. "There are a lot of cameras here."

"It's so weird, though. Somebody unplugged the recorder. Nothing has taped since midnight. I'll try to get it started again, but hey—for minimum wage, I'm not all that motivated to figure it out. If anybody asks, though, I remember your car: a white Chevy half-ton with Utah plates."

Slater eyed him. "Thanks."

"More like thank you—for doing what I wish I could do."

Red-hat groaned and lifted his arm.

"Should I call an ambulance?" the kid asked.

"Don't bother. He's coming around."

Slater climbed in the Thunderbird and drove

away. Arizona was decidedly redneck, but at least the speed limits were high, and he put the town far behind him.

———•———

The countryside was beautiful here, and as the light shifted, he felt more awake. He crossed into New Mexico, with no appreciable shift in the landscape but better road surfaces. Driving back roads was more interesting than the monotonous freeway, and it gave him time to think, first about Steve and Lillian and the necklace, and then about Conrad and Doris. Even now he could feel his face burning just thinking about them conspiring, and he ran through some ideas, some scenarios that might quash their mini cabal.

The landscape flattened out for a few hours, then became mountainous again as he approached the ranch. He watched the map on his phone as the last turn approached, off the ragged pavement onto a dirt road through the scrubby desert. If anyone was outdoors, they'd see him coming—there was no way to drive this road without kicking up plumes of dust. Soon he crossed a barbed-wire fence line with a cattle guard across the road, rumbling under his tires. This was probably the boundary of Steve's land.

In a couple of miles, right where Jeff's map marker said it would be, he arrived at a set of structures—a sprawling house flanked by several outbuildings. The only vehicle in the dusty yard was a white Camry with New Mexico plates. Slater pulled up quietly behind it and killed the engine. He sat for a minute, silence pounding in his ears after so many hours on the road, taking in the scene.

The outbuildings looked weather-beaten, but the house was in good shape, modern windows and adobe shingles. In Cali they used those to lessen the threat from wildfires, but he couldn't imagine that was an issue here, with so little vegetation. There were a couple of trees in the yard, some kind of pine, though he'd never seen that species before. The quality of the light was different too—it was too bright, the sky too pale. Climbing out, he inhaled sharply at the blast of cold air and silently closed the car door. He could see his breath, and he kicked himself again for not bringing any warm clothes.

The Camry had a rental company sticker in the window, he saw, and its presence implied someone was here. He could poke around the outbuildings or walk behind the house, as there were no fences to discourage that. But was he thinking rationally? He felt punch-drunk from all the driving. Maybe he should just bang on the door.

The decision was made for him, however—the front door swung open, and Steve stepped onto the porch, hands on his hips.

"Can I help you?" Steve called to him.

"I'm so glad you're here," Slater blurted out, stepping around the Camry.

"Slater?" He shaded his eyes with his hand against the bright sun, peering out at him. "What are you doing here?"

"You weren't answering your phone. Are you alone?"

"Of course I'm alone."

"You took the train, didn't you."

"The *Southwest Chief.* How did you know that?"

"Your Lexus is parked under Union Station."

"I can't believe you found it. Damn, you're good."

Slater took a few steps toward the house. "What happened in your bedroom at home?"

Steve didn't reply right away. "I came out here to be alone," he said finally. "You can turn around and go back the way you came."

"Where's Lillian?"

"She's not home? I thought maybe she told you where to find me."

"She's gone missing, the same as you."

"So you didn't hear her side of it."

"Is she still alive, Steve? Not in the trunk of the Camry, or planted out here in a shallow grave?"

"Are you kidding me?" he demanded. "She's my wife."

"Exactly."

Slater knew he wasn't that guy, but his words had the desired effect.

"Who even suggested that?" Steve demanded. "I'd never do that. She's probably off on one of her excursions." He glared at Slater, then said, "What were you doing in my bedroom?"

"I've been driving all night, and I haven't had anything but water to drink. I feel like I might fall over. Can I get horizontal for a minute? Then we can talk."

Steve watched him for a moment, then said, "Fine."

Slater followed him inside, where it was much warmer, thankfully, and into a bedroom, twice the size of his own, with a neatly made bed.

"The bathroom's through there," Steve said, gesturing to a doorway, then left, closing the door behind him.

The window looked onto the yard, where both cars were visible. Slater unlatched the sash and slid it open a crack so that he'd hear the Camry if it started. He unbuckled his belt and took off his boots, setting them at the ready beside the bed, then stretched out. Looking at his phone, he set the alarm for an hour, then put it beside his head.

TEN

Tires crunching on gravel woke him. That was important, he knew, but he had to think about where he was. Daylight, a warm bed with floral sheets, a cold draft. It all snapped into his mind at once, and he sat up, stepping into his boots and tightening his belt as he went to the window.

A new-looking gray F150 was pulling past his car, its diesel engine chugging. It stopped in front of a structure across the yard, the building with big doors—a barn, maybe, or a garage. The engine died and a guy climbed out, wearing work boots and jeans and a puffy orange vest, gray hair sprouting from beneath his ball cap. Moving leisurely, he was digging for something in the bed of the truck. Not a threat, Slater decided, and definitely not from LA.

Walking out into the house, he realized he felt better, less strung out from highway hypnosis. The place had airy high ceilings, Mexican tile floors, great light. The quiet here was so unfamiliar that it was distracting, a roar in his ears. He found Steve sitting cross-legged on the sofa in the living room, facing a big picture window that looked out onto the rolling landscape. It would be very easy to sit here and look at that all day, Slater thought, taking it in.

"I was going to wake you soon," Steve said, looking up as he approached.

"Who's the cowboy in the pickup?"

"It must be Tom. I heard a diesel engine."

"It's an F150. It looks like he's going to work in the barn."

"Tom rents the water rights from me, and keeps an eye on the place when I'm not here."

Uncle Tom, Jeff had called him, Slater remembered.

There was a sharp knock on the door, and Steve rose.

"Mind your manners with this guy," Steve said quietly. "Small-town people do things differently."

"Maybe I'll just stay out of sight."

"You can't. He's seen your car. If you hide, he'll think I've got a woman in here."

"I can think of worse things," Slater said, but

followed him to the door.

Steve pulled it open and greeted Tom with a loud exchange of words and a bro hug. Tom was maybe in his sixties, his face lined with age and sun exposure.

"This is Slater, from Los Angeles," Steve said.

Tom gave him a subtle once-over. "You're driving the T-bird? That's a great car. I had one back in the day, a little older than yours. I loved the power."

"I feel it when gas prices jump, though," Slater said, meeting his eye. And there it was—that vibe, that longing, so hard to conceal. He could feel it in this guy.

Tom laughed nervously and looked away. "I wanted to talk business," he said to Steve.

"Come inside," Steve said, and led him to the living room.

Slater found the kitchen, where he ate a banana and some bread, half listening to their talk. It wasn't important, though, so he checked his phone, leaning on the kitchen island. Surprisingly there was cell service out here, but no messages that he needed to deal with.

Eventually Tom left, the front door slamming behind him, and Slater headed into the living room. Steve was on the sofa again.

"It was Jeff, wasn't it, who let you into my house," Steve said, turning to look at him.

"He called me to come and see the mess," Slater said, standing behind the sofa. "He thought you'd been kidnapped."

"I never intended that. I guess I should have called him."

"So what did you intend?" Slater demanded.

"I needed space to think." He frowned. "Would you sit down? You're making me nervous, looming over me like that."

"You should be nervous," Slater said, moving to a nearby chair. "If I wasn't so tired, I would have smacked you around already."

"Why would you do that? I'm not the bad guy."

Slater threw up his hands. "So enlighten me."

Steve sighed. "It was me who tore up the closet. I found the necklace."

Slater nodded, struggling not to smile. Just like that, the truth. It had been an inside job all along. And Steve was such a boy scout that he couldn't even lie about it.

"That was a surprise to you, that Lillian still had it?"

"Of course it was," he said sharply.

"Where is it now?" Slater asked.

"It's safe."

"Here?" Slater said, raising his eyebrows.

Steve sighed and looked to the window. "It's here."

"Does Lillian know you found it?"

"She was there," he said, emphatic again.

"You confronted her?"

"She heard me searching for it, I guess, and came in. We fought." He met Slater's eye. "Verbally, I mean. I felt so betrayed."

"How did you leave things?" Slater said, watching him closely.

"I wouldn't let her take the necklace. She stormed out, and I threw some stuff in an overnight bag and came here. I needed to think."

"What made you decide to toss her closet?"

"It was a silly idea," Steve said, looking away. "Just a hunch."

"Sing, brother," Slater said sharply, "or I really will rough you up."

"Good god, man—you need to relax." He watched Slater for a moment before he spoke. "When you interviewed Carolina, she remembered that Silvana Lee wore a Clytemnestra scarf. Lillian loves those. It struck me that maybe she was collaborating with this Silvana Lee."

Slater frowned. "So you tore apart her stuff because they wear the same scarf?"

"I know it sounds tenuous." He sighed. "I guess it was kind of a cumulative thing. She's always been more concerned about money than about people. Vegas—she loves that place, like an addict. I like nice things, but family, friends, staff are way more important."

"So you got suspicious."

"And I was right." He gazed out the window. "Not about Silvana Lee, but about the necklace. It hadn't been stolen at all—she still had it."

Slater rubbed his eyes. "When Lillian left, she took her car?"

Steve thought for a second. "Yeah."

"Have you talked to anyone else since then?"

"I should have called Jeff. I left a message at the office that I wouldn't be in."

"That's the only reason nobody called the cops," Slater said.

"I didn't mean to upset anyone," he said, frowning. "I just needed to decompress, get some sleep, think things through."

"You keep saying that. Have you had enough thinking time?"

"Does it matter?"

"The longer you stay here, avoiding her, the likelier it is that she'll get away with it."

"I'm sorry, but I can't even deal with that yet."

"You have to, man," Slater said intently. "The other day you were complaining about your son not taking responsibility. Right now you're doing it your damn self."

"She's my wife."

Slater shook his head impatiently. "Doesn't matter."

"I don't want to hurt her," he said, face

contorting, his tone pleading.

Slater closed his eyes for a second, trying to suppress his gut reaction, but he just couldn't do it. He rose and stepped over to Steve, standing over him and slapping him across the face, open-handed, and then back on the other side—a firm kovac.

"What was that for?" Steve demanded, leaning away and glaring at him, holding his palm to his cheek.

"You need to snap out of it," Slater said, stepping back.

Even now, he didn't look fearful, Slater saw, just startled, and a little angry. Deep down, despite the dithering, he was a stable guy.

"I can't just change the way I feel," Steve said.

"I just did it for you, though—you're not whining anymore."

"You can't just walk into my house and smack me around. I don't care what your interest in this is."

Slater held up his palms. "I'll try not to do that again, if you try to be rational."

"That's asking a lot. I love her, Slater. Love isn't rational."

"You're being sentimental. It has nothing to do with reality."

"What would you have me do?" Steve demanded.

Slater dropped back into his chair. "Two things. One I'm going to make you do. The other is up to you."

"OK," he said evenly, concern in his eyes.

"First, you have to turn in the necklace."

"I was thinking about that. Maybe we could just rescind the insurance claim. Your people haven't paid out on it yet."

"No way," Slater said, shaking his head. "That ship has sailed. You reported it to the cops, and the company is already invested in the claim—they're paying me to look into it."

"Maybe if I paid them for those expenses, and explained that it was a mistake."

"It's not negotiable," Slater said, holding his gaze. "You're going to turn it in. You have to."

"What's the other thing?"

"You take steps to make sure Lillian doesn't do it again. It's not just insurance fraud—she's ripping you off. If we wrote everything up properly, I bet we could get her locked up for four to six years. But that's not my call. You're the one who can make that happen." He added, "I'll help you, of course."

"Why wouldn't you just report her to the cops?"

"You want me to do the dirty work, is that it?" Slater said sharply.

"Isn't it kind of your job?"

Slater scoffed. "All I do all day long is deal with lowlifes—crooks and liars and chiselers. I don't give a damn what happens to Lillian, and I don't care about Cudahy Mutual's profit margins. I'm not going to help her rip off the company, but I'm also not going to help them punish her, unless there's some impetus. And that has to come from you."

"You missed one thing," Steve said, watching him.

Slater threw up his hands. "What's that?"

"You didn't say that you don't care what happens to me."

"That is an interesting omission." He watched Steve for a moment, then sat back in the chair and looked out at the landscape. "I can see why you bought here. It really is beautiful."

"It's not a whole lot of land, compared to some of the neighbors," Steve said, "but it certainly isn't crowded. You can't beat that view."

Still gazing out the window, Slater said, "I think you might be the first non-lowlife I've worked with in a long time. It's actually kind of liberating that I don't want to break your jaw."

"I'm not so sure about that—I feel like a lowlife, not being able to turn her in. I'm not so different from Lillian."

"You were going to do the right thing with the necklace, though," Slater said, meeting his gaze. "That's why you brought it with you. I know you were—I can feel it. All that talk about walking back the insurance claim. You wouldn't have even tried that. You want to protect her, but not rip anyone off."

"Probably not," Steve said quietly.

"Tell me what you want to do about Lillian. How things go from here depends on that. You have to decide now."

"I don't want her to get in trouble, or go to jail. She's weak, Slater. She—"

"Spare me the explanations," Slater said, raising a hand. "So if we're not turning her in, I need to come up with a plan to turn the necklace over to Cudahy Mutual."

"Why the insurance company?" Steve asked. "Why not the police?"

"The cops would ask a lot of questions, and demand explanations. 'Where has it been, who's been in possession, how long have you had it?' The insurance company only wants the goods, then they'll back off. If we're doing this without incriminating her, or you, or me, it can't be the cops."

"OK." Steve nodded. "I get it."

"The upside is that Cudahy Mutual will just hand it back to you because they haven't paid the claim yet. They will jack your premiums, however."

"It sounds like a bit of rigmarole, but if you think it's necessary."

"Does Lillian know you took the necklace with you?"

"It would be a reasonable assumption," Steve said. "She left screaming because I wouldn't let her have it. I was afraid she was going to try to sell it, or break it apart and sell the stones."

"She would have, eventually," Slater said. "Give me the necklace."

Steve eyed him. "Are you sure I shouldn't hang onto it?"

"You don't get to distrust me," Slater said, raising his voice. "I'm the one holding all the cards. You piss me off, and I'll put Lillian and you both behind bars so fast it'll make your head spin."

"Jesus, you're so sensitive," Steve said, frowning and rising from the sofa.

He walked across the room toward the fireplace, a massive fieldstone structure that tapered toward the ceiling. Halfway to it, he peered into the foyer, ducking to see out the window to the yard.

"Tom's not hanging around, is he?" Steve said.

Slater went into the foyer and looked out. "He's doing something with a roll of wire over by the barn."

Stepping back into the main room, Slater watched as Steve stood at the fireplace and grasped an oval-shaped white stone, near the side, at shoulder height. It slipped out easily, not attached to the mortar. He reached into the void it left and pulled out a dark-blue velvet bag.

"Catch," Steve said, and tossed it underhand to Slater.

Slater snagged it out of the air. It was heavier than he'd expected. Loosening the drawstring, he pulled out the necklace, draping it over his palm. It was huge, and so much grander in person than in the insurance photos. He wasn't really into bling, but this piece was eye-catching. Hypnotic, even. So sparkly, it held his eyes with the gravity of something rare.

"Want to try it on?" Steve asked, raising his eyebrows.

"It's not really my style, but I totally understand why someone would wear it. You'd be the focus of attention in any room you walked into. Did you pick it out, or did Lillian?"

"She had it designed."

Slater took a last look, then dropped it back into the bag, rubbing it to wipe off his fingerprints. His DNA was all over it now too, but if things worked out, that wouldn't matter.

"It's time to head back," Slater said.

Steve turned from the fireplace, where he'd replaced the loose stone, looking startled. "Today? The *Southwest Chief* isn't until later tonight."

"Screw the train. I'll drive."

"But the train is so relaxing. I sleep like a baby."

"There's no time for that," Slater said impatiently.

Steve sighed. "All right. I have a couple of things to do here, and I have to drop the car in Gallup."

"Is there any food?"

"Good idea. We'll eat before we leave."

Slater headed out the front door. It was still cold but not as biting with the afternoon sun overhead. Walking to his car, he looked around for Tom, and saw movement over where he'd parked his truck, inside the barn, the big doors propped open now. Opening the trunk of the Thunderbird, Slater loosened the wing nut holding down the plate over the spare tire, then lifted it up and set the blue velvet bag in the space underneath. He gently eased the plate down again, making sure it wasn't crushing the valuable piece. It fit, and the bag wasn't visible. After he tightened the nut again, he slammed the lid.

The barn had a dirt floor and served as a workshop rather than anything to do with animals, judging by the tools lining the walls, Slater saw, strolling inside. Lumber was piled at one side next to a little tractor, and a long workbench ran along the opposite wall. Tom had leather gloves on, lifting a coil of wire to hang it on a spike a few feet above his head. Slater admired his body. Even with the puffy winter vest, he could tell the guy was buff, from manual labor rather than hanging around a gym. Completing his task, he turned as Slater walked in, pulling off his gloves.

"It's a long drive from California," he said, flashing a toothy smile.

"Once you're out of LA there's nobody on the roads, so it's pretty painless," Slater said. "So you're an actual cowboy?"

Tom adjusted his cap higher on his head, assessing Slater. "I'm a cattleman. Cowboys work for guys like me."

"Your land is nearby?"

"About five miles farther up the highway. I'm Steve's closest neighbor."

"You must get lonely out here," he said, raising his eyebrows and casually rubbing his crotch.

Tom's eyes narrowed. "I suppose that's true."

Slater stepped closer and took hold of the lapels of his vest, pulling them apart. "You're in amazing shape."

"What's happening right now?" Tom said, frozen in place, his chest heaving.

"What do you want to happen?" Slater said, and moved closer, hesitating just before their lips met, waiting for Tom to make the last move.

Tom kissed him, finally, leaning in like he was collapsing, the tension melting out of his body. His mouth tasted like something tangy, maybe tobacco, but at least he was good at it. Slater ran his hand into his hair, and Tom tentatively groped his jeans, pulling him closer. Slater could feel the guy's stiff cock, his luxuriously warm body.

"Come over here," Slater said, pulling away and stepping toward the workbench.

"What if Steve comes in?" Tom asked quietly, glancing toward the yard, but followed him.

"He's not going to do that. He's working at his desk or something."

Slater positioned him against the workbench and pushed his orange vest off, then unbuttoned his shirt. Tom had beautiful pecs, sprouting gray hair, and Slater tongued his nipples, eliciting a gasp. Reaching down, he unbuckled Tom's belt and pulled out his cock, which got harder as Slater manipulated it, leaning in and kissing his neck. This wasn't going to take long, as Tom was close, Slater could tell—panting, his head back, eyes closed.

"Look at me," Slater demanded, and Tom met his eye. Slater locked his mouth to Tom's, probing with his tongue, stroking his cock, and felt Tom's body tense and vibrate as he came. Slater held him until the spasms subsided. Tom leaned forward and groped at Slater's cock through his jeans.

Slater started to unbuckle his pants, and Tom dropped to his knees, unbidden, pulling off his cap, to take him into his mouth. He was inexperienced, but enthusiastic, and Slater guided him with his fingertips, and soon came, grabbing his head to stop him. Tom rose and wrapped his arms around Slater, leaning on the workbench, and they stood that way for a minute, Slater enjoying the warmth, the intimacy, breathing in the scent of his hair.

"How long are you around for?" Tom asked finally.

"I'm taking Steve back to LA tonight. I came out to get him."

"That's too bad," he said, pulling back. "He just got here."

Slater buckled his belt. "He's in trouble, Tom. Real trouble."

Tom's eyes grew wide. "Really? What kind of trouble?"

He looked pointedly toward the open doors and lowered his voice. "I'm sure you can imagine."

Tom stared at him for a second. "Trouble with the law?"

Most people could imagine much worse—the mob, drug cartels, even an unhinged jilted lover—but Slater could work with it. He nodded gravely. "I can't share the details, but I know I can trust you with this. You'd be doing us both a big favor if you kept quiet about seeing him here."

"You want me to lie to the police?" he said, pronouncing it like a Southerner, "*poh*-lease."

"Of course not," Slater said, waving dismissively.

"But maybe you can just say, sure, you've seen him, but you don't remember which weekend it was. They should be asking him, right, not you."

"It sounds serious," he said, and looked thoughtful. "Steve's always been a good neighbor. I'll keep it to myself."

"Excellent," Slater said. "He'll tell you all about it once it's sorted out. And maybe I'll come out here again someday, and you and I can do some other stuff."

Tom blushed and smiled broadly. "I'd like that."

"See you around, cattle man," he said, and went back to the house.

Steve was standing at the island in the kitchen, slicing a baguette.

"What were you up to?" Steve asked, looking him over. "Your jeans are all dirty."

Slater looked down and slapped away the dust. "Helping Tom with some stuff."

Steve frowned. "Really?"

They heard the sound of the diesel engine start up.

"It sounds like he's leaving," Steve said, and gestured to the food he'd put out. "Help yourself."

They stood at the island to eat, Slater scarfing down fruit and tomatoes, Steve more methodically eating cheese and bread. It took him a while to collect his things and close up the house, and

Slater's phone said it was almost five when Steve finally appeared, wearing a luxe short leather jacket and carrying his shoulder bag.

"I'm ready," he said cheerfully. "Do you want to lead the way? The rental place is right by the train station in Gallup."

"I'll follow you," Slater said.

Steve locked the front door and threw his bag into the backseat of the Camry.

"It's about ninety minutes' drive," he said, pulling open the driver's door.

"Turn on your phone," Slater said.

"I'd rather not," he said, his brow furrowing. "It'll blow up with Carolina trying to talk to me about work, and I really don't want to deal with Lillian yet."

"Fine, but turn it on if you lose sight of me behind you."

Slater climbed into the Thunderbird and waited for Steve to pull out, following him slowly along the dirt road to the highway. The shadows were growing long, and Slater switched on his headlights.

Once they were on the highway, Steve wasn't moving very fast. Exactly fifty-five, Slater realized, glancing at his speedometer. Who does that? He let it go for a while, but eventually couldn't stand it anymore. Pulling up on Steve's bumper, he flashed his lights and swerved from side to side.

Steve turned on his hazard flashers and slowed, pulling onto the shoulder, and stepped out of the car. Slater climbed out too.

"What's wrong?" Steve asked, looking worried.

"You're driving like my grandmother. Can you speed it up a little?"

"That's why you stopped me? I thought my trunk was on fire. I'm driving the speed limit, Slater. I don't want to get in trouble."

"I'll make you a deal: if you get a citation, I'll pay it."

"OK," he said, dubious. "But they have speed limits for a reason, you know."

"Just drive," Slater demanded, and climbed back into his car.

Steve pulled back onto the highway, and soon they were traveling faster, exactly five miles per hour over the limit. It was frustrating, but Slater knew he had to let it go, focusing instead on the dramatic shifting colors of the Southwestern sunset filling the sky.

ELEVEN

ell after dark, Slater followed the Camry into a parking lot with a rental-car logo emblazoned on the squat little office. The place looked closed, but he watched as Steve pulled his bag out of the back and then dropped the car keys into a slot in the door. Walking back to the Thunderbird and pulling open the passenger door, he threw his bag and his jacket behind the seat and climbed in.

"Road trip," Steve said. "Woo-hoo!"

Slater watched him, eyes narrowing. "You're a very upbeat person."

"Come on—it's Saturday night, and we're getting on the open road."

"With ten hours of driving ahead of us," he said, pulling the gearshift down into Drive and heading out of the lot.

"So you're a glass-half-empty kind of guy, I take it."

Slater crossed the tracks and accelerated onto the freeway.

"When I was finished college," Steve said, "I wanted to bring my car home to LA, so I drove it across the country. I took back roads the whole way. You see so much more."

"I've noticed that," Slater said.

"At one point I was taking a break in the desert somewhere here in New Mexico. I was stretched out on the hood of my car, enjoying the sun. Across the road there was one of those green signs, pointing to two towns in opposite directions. I forget what they were, but I remember thinking, I can go anywhere, do anything. Pick either direction at random. I could go somewhere I'd never been, and reinvent myself. That's what I'm talking about—the freedom of the open road."

"Why didn't you?"

"Well, I had obligations in LA. My plan was to work with my dad. Don't get me wrong—I have no regrets about going into the family business. But I still remember that feeling, the unlimited possibilities."

"So maybe it's OK if your son makes that choice," Slater said, "to live out his own possibilities."

Steve scoffed. "That's different."

"That feeling—is it why you bought land out here?"

"Maybe. I've always had a soft spot for this part of the world."

They rode in silence for a while, until Slater pulled off the freeway.

"I need gas," he explained, turning into a brightly lit station.

"Let me buy it," Steve said.

"Why would you do that?"

"You're kind of helping me. Or at least doing things the way I want."

"Sure, I'll take your gas money," Slater said, pulling up to a pump. "Buy me an apple when you're in there."

They both climbed out, and Slater loosened the gas cap. Watching Steve walk inside, waiting for the pump to turn on, he wondered if they sold booze. It didn't really matter, as he couldn't drink now anyway. The pump hummed to life, and after he'd fueled up, Steve came back, tossing him an apple.

"Do you want me to drive?"

"That would be great," Slater said, and got in the passenger seat.

It felt weird to be on this side, a powerless observer, and he watched as Steve shifted the seat position and adjusted the rearview mirror.

"There's almost no one else on the planet that I'd let drive my car," Slater said. "But I know how conscientious you are."

Steve chuckled and confidently started the engine, then pulled the gear shift into Drive.

"This thing certainly has guts," he said, accelerating onto the freeway.

"Just don't get pulled over."

Munching on his apple, Slater reached into the backseat and found his atlas, a thick coil-bound book, then clicked on the dome light and flipped through the pages.

"Paper maps. That's old school," Steve said, glancing at it. "I know a couple of back roads to get us down to the 10. One goes through Phoenix, and the other through Flagstaff and then south."

"Stay on the 40," Slater said, studying the map. "We're taking a side trip before we hit the 15."

"Seriously? To where?"

"The Mojave National Preserve," Slater said, and clicked off the light.

"OK," he said, and added, "Is that near Vegas? We could do a detour. It's the kind of place that's open twenty-four hours."

"We're definitely not going there. Guys like me don't do well in Vegas."

Steve looked at him. "Vegas was built for guys like you."

"Exactly," Slater said, and reclined his seat-back, shifting to get comfortable. "Wake me when we get to civilization."

"You mean the next big town? That's Flagstaff."

"I mean Cali."

"The first place in California on this road is Needles. The *Southwest Chief* stops there, but I wouldn't say it's especially civilized. It's in a much drier desert than where my ranch is."

"Sounds like paradise," Slater said, and folded his arms, willing himself to sleep.

Waking under bright fluorescent lighting, he felt cold, and the smell of leather was in his nose. He sat up, and found a black jacket draped over him. Why was he on the passenger side of his own car? Steve pulled open the driver's door and climbed in, handing Slater a plastic bag.

"What's going on?" Slater demanded, his tongue thick from sleep.

"I stopped for gas. You looked cold, so I gave you my jacket. I got you another apple and some peanuts for later."

Slater rubbed his eyes. "Where are we?"

"Flagstaff, baby. The bright lights."

"I have to pee," Slater said, handing him the jacket and pulling the door handle. He paused, eyeing the keys in the ignition, but then quashed the urge to grab them before he left. Steve was not going to steal his car.

On his way out through the gas station's mini market, he saw they had booze for sale—beer in the cooler, hard liquor behind the counter.

"Give me a pint of the bourbon," he said to the clerk, dropping a twenty on the counter and watching as she wrapped it in a paper bag and made change.

Slater climbed into the car to find Steve holding something half-eaten and wrapped in foil, filling the air with the smell of grease and microwaved death.

"What did you buy?" Steve asked, through a mouthful of food.

"Tampons," Slater said flatly.

"That's a flask," he said. "I can tell. Are you planning on getting drunk?"

"Fuck off, Steve," he said, and put the bottle in the glove compartment.

Reclining in his seat and folding his arms, Slater closed his eyes, ending the discussion.

———◆———

He woke again at another gas station. Steve was filling the tank, and Slater climbed out to stretch in the cold air. Checking his phone, it was after eleven, and the map said they were in Needles.

There was a text from Max:

Guess who just got home?

Slater phoned him, and when he picked up, said, "You saw her?"

"Just for a second on the video," Max said. "It was really grainy in the dim light, but I'm sure it was her. There was a lot of hair."

"Is she still there?"

"She is, but she hasn't been back into the kitchen. Do you want me to sit on the place? I'm thinking she's in for the night, but I could go first thing tomorrow."

"Don't bother," Slater said. "We know now that she's using the apartment. But let me know if she leaves."

"Where are you?"

"Needles. I'll be home in the morning."

Slater watched Steve put the nozzle away and pull his receipt out of the pump. When he'd ended the call, he asked, "Ready to switch?"

"Happy to," Steve said, and walked around to the passenger side.

Slater climbed in and spent a minute moving the seat, then finding a marker on the map on his phone. Like the marker for Steve's ranch, it was a dot in the middle of nowhere. He set it as their destination before steering the Thunderbird back onto the freeway. Steve cranked the seat back up, clearly not tired from all the driving. They traveled in silence for a while, until Steve spoke.

"What would I do without her?" he said.

Slater looked at him, but it was hard to see his expression in the dark. "You mean Lillian?"

"Of course I mean Lillian. And don't try to slap me again—I'm being as rational as I can, and you need to keep your eyes on the road."

Slater grinned to himself. "How long have you known her?"

"Her grandparents and mine were interned together in Arizona during the war. Our families go way back."

"Is that how you met?"

"My parents set us up," Steve said. "With older people there's still a cultural habit of doing arranged introductions, but I married her because I loved her."

"I hear that word every freaking day, but I have no idea what it's supposed to mean," Slater said.

"Love?"

"It sounds like an entanglement. Like, 'My shoe is caught in the storm grate.' And getting married—you have to think of it like a business deal, not some fairy tale. If it's not working out, sever the contract."

"That's so callous. What would our families think?"

"You can't live your life for your family," Slater said.

"What would you do, in my shoes?"

"You've got me there. I can't even imagine the things that straight people do."

Steve laughed. "That is such a lie. It's not that different."

"Maybe not," Slater said. "OK—I'd kick her out of my house, get a lawyer to negotiate a divorce, and marry Carolina."

"Carolina? Where the hell did that come from?"

"She's hot, you may have noticed. And you seem to trust her."

"All true. But Carolina?"

"Do you trust Lillian?" Slater asked, and got no reply. "So there you go. You're a decent person, Steve, but you're enmeshed with someone who's not."

"Are you a licensed counselor, or is this just pro bono armchair analysis?" Steve demanded.

"It's impossible to be objective about yourself. Everyone is a jumble of contradictions—I can see yours more easily than my own."

"Like loving a woman that I don't trust."

"And also the fact that you know what unlimited potential tastes like," Slater said, "but you don't want your son to try it."

Steve was quiet for a while, both of them

watching the bright lines on the asphalt, the red pinpoints of tail lights far ahead.

"As a gay guy, could you tell Jeff is gay too?" Steve asked quietly.

"I had some sense of that," Slater said. In his mind flashed the memory of fucking Jeff on his baseball duvet under the heavy-metal posters, the smell of his hair. "So how did you figure out that I'm gay?"

"Carolina saw you checking out my butt, and she said you never once looked at her cleavage. She has a great body, like you said."

"Good to know you're not blind."

"It's not that I want Jeff to limit himself, but I worry about him, and the path he'll take."

"He's going to make a great husband for somebody—the same as you," Slater said. "But it'll be a guy."

"You can see into the future now?"

"I can see his character. He's completely stable, and straightforward. A straight arrow. He probably got it by osmosis, watching you."

"I hope you're right," Steve said. "But why would you think I'm a good husband? Lillian has never been happy."

"Well, I know you're an open book, and I know you're loyal. Stupidly loyal, considering the woman is screwing you over."

Steve sighed. "But you think Jeff will snag a

decent man."

"He's totally hot, and he has good manners. He'll have his pick."

"I'm glad you think he's good-looking. It's hard to be objective about that too."

"It runs in the family," Slater said.

"You think I'm hot," Steve said, sitting up. "I knew it. That is so flattering."

"It's even hotter that you kind of don't know that you are. I'd fuck you in a second if you were into it." He looked at Steve. "I'll pull this car over right now."

Steve laughed. "Too bad I'm straight."

"Like you said, it's not that different. I could do things to you that Lillian never dreamed of."

"I bet you could."

"Have you ever kissed a guy?" Slater asked.

"It's not going to happen, Romeo," he said firmly. "Cool your jets."

Slater chuckled. "Lots of straight guys mess around, though. How about your neighbor Tom—do you think he's totally straight?"

"I never thought about it. It's kind of the default setting out there." He was quiet for a moment. "You're not going to tell me he's not? Oh, my god, did you have sex with him?"

"Would that be shocking?"

"Actually, yes," Steve said, looking at him intently.

"Then consider it bullshit. I went out to the barn and hit on him, and he reacted the way you did."

"That sounds a lot more plausible." He sat back. "Phew—I can feel the planet returning to a stable orbit again."

Slater didn't need to out Tom, he thought, watching the broken white line flash in the glare of his headlights. Conrad had once said only knuckleheads kiss and tell, and based on how Steve had reacted, that must be a reasonable maxim.

"When you showed up at the ranch," Steve said, "you kind of said you were impaired because you hadn't had anything to drink. When I saw you bought the pint, I realized you were talking about liquor. Most people think of it the other way around—the liquor makes you impaired."

"I usually have a drink in the evening. Instead I drove all night."

"Do you drink a lot?"

"Not a lot."

"But you bought that pint," Steve said, tapping the glove compartment, "even though you were getting behind the wheel."

"It's for later," Slater said irritably.

"Still, it sounds like it's interfering with your life. That's the definition of a drinking problem."

"I don't have a problem," Slater said. "I've got

a handle on when and where and how much I drink. It's all figured out."

"I know some people who are in AA. I could get one of them to take you to a meeting."

"I don't need you messing with my life," Slater shouted.

"OK," he said, and sighed, and sat back.

Did he actually think that because they were stuck in a car together for a few hours that he could serve up that kind of advice? Why did so many people try to do that? There was a long list, stretching way back—Doris, from the moment he'd been born, and then teachers, counselors, shrinks, even freaking Conrad. He just wanted to be left alone. Why was that so hard to accept?

———◆———

Before long, Slater slowed to take an exit ramp.

"Kelso?" Steve said, reading the road sign. "Is that our side trip?"

Slater braked and eased the car over a cattle guard, which rattled beneath the tires.

"A little farther than that," he said.

"What's farther than Kelso?"

"You'll see when we get there."

Steve sighed. "So mysterious. I'm going to try to sleep."

Slater drove hard on the narrow two-lane road, the empty desert invisible in the darkness stretching all around. Steve stirred and mumbled when the car rumbled across the rail tracks at Kelso. The lights of the hamlet receding in the mirror, Slater built up speed again.

Soon they were at the marker on his phone map. Slater slowed to a stop and pulled onto the shoulder, killing the lights and scooping up the device, pocketing it.

"Where are we?" Steve asked, sitting up. "It's pitch-black."

"The Mojave Desert," Slater said, and climbed out.

"That's not very specific."

It was cold, but thankfully not windy, and Slater opened the trunk and put on his work gloves. Pulling out the shovel, he set it against the bumper, then unscrewed the wing nut holding down the plate over the spare tire, extracting the blue velvet bag and its weighty contents. It was too big to fit in the pockets of his jeans. He was going to have to carry it. Steve was standing a few feet away, his jacket on, watching him.

"You carry the shovel," Slater said, slamming the trunk and plunging them into darkness.

Steve didn't move. "Are you armed?" he asked quietly.

"No. Let's go," he said, and started walking away from the road, into the blackness.

Steve stood where he was, a vague silhouette

against the sky when Slater looked back.

"Don't you trust me, Steve?"

"Of course I don't bloody trust you. We're in the middle of nowhere in the middle of the night, and you want me to carry a shovel out into the desert."

"We're going to need it to bury the necklace."

"Bury it? Why?" he demanded. "Why here?"

"Plausible deniability," Slater said, and started walking again.

"Don't you have a flashlight?" Steve called after him.

"Your eyes will get better night vision soon. Just step around the bushes. You'll be fine."

Steve's shoes crunched on the dirt behind him as he caught up and then walked abreast.

"You're right," he said, after a few minutes. "I'm starting to see more. It's amazing that you can see by ambient starlight. So how far are we going?"

"Have you heard of the ninety-ten rule?"

"What's that?"

"Ninety percent of the people who go into the wilderness and get out of their car never stray more than ten minutes from it. We have to go well past the ten-minute limit."

"Why not walk ten minutes from the 40?" Steve asked, stepping away to avoid a low yucca. "It runs through the same desert."

"There are way more people around the freeway. Nobody comes out here—there's no off-roading, no hiking trails anywhere nearby."

"So we could go anywhere isolated—but you had this spot programmed into your GPS."

"It's mathematically extremely unlikely to be visited," Slater said.

"You just had that picked out and waiting in your phone? Why?"

Slater didn't answer him.

"I get it," he said. "Lowlife-type stuff."

"How about we just listen to the desert for a while?" Slater said, and they walked in silence.

Finally Slater stopped, and dropped the necklace on the ground.

"Here," he said, and took the shovel from Steve, and started digging.

"Need a hand?" Steve asked, watching him.

Slater ignored him, grunting with the effort, and soon had dug down a couple of feet. Scooping up the necklace, he dropped it unceremoniously into the hole and started filling it again.

"Are you sure it's not going to get washed away in a flash flood?" Steve said. "It's rainy season."

After he'd replaced all the dirt and smoothed the surface, Slater stabbed the shovel into the earth right above the necklace and stood erect, stretching his back.

"We crossed the arroyo back beside the

highway," he said. "This is high ground."

"If you say so."

"Look away," Slater said, pulling off his gloves and stuffing them in his back pocket.

Steve didn't budge, hesitating before he spoke. "What are you going to do?"

"Turn on my phone," Slater said impatiently. "It'll ruin my night vision, but it doesn't have to ruin yours."

"Why do you need your phone?" he asked, turning his back.

"To get the precise location of where we're standing." Wincing at the stab of light as the screen lit up, he opened an app that gave him precise latitude and longitude, and took a screen shot. Next he photographed the shovel from three directions, capturing the layout of the nearby bushes in blinding flashes of white light.

"You can look now," Slater said, slipping his phone into his jeans. "Can you pull out the shovel and smooth the dirt? I'm basically blind right now."

Not able to watch, he listened to the sound of metal tamping earth.

"That's as good as I can get it," Steve said finally.

"Back to the car, then," he said. "Do you know the way?"

"How would I know that?" Steve demanded.

"You led us out here."

"Cover your eyes for a second," Slater said, and checked his phone, setting it to navigate back to where he'd parked. Switching it off again, he pointed out the direction. "I'll follow right behind you until I can see again."

Steve set off, with Slater echoing his steps.

"How does this equate to turning in the necklace to the insurance company?" Steve asked. "Only you and I know where it is."

"Do you actually know?" Slater asked. "Could you and Lillian drive out here tomorrow and dig it up?"

Steve went a few paces before he replied. "Good point. So you don't actually trust me."

"Not where Lillian is concerned, no."

"Why are we doing this?" Steve demanded.

"I can report to Cudahy Mutual that I got an anonymous tip with the necklace's location, and let them retrieve it. That way, it's not connected to me."

"Except that you drove right by here."

"I did not," Slater said.

"Well, you definitely drove out to New Mexico."

"No, I didn't. No one saw me there."

"Tom did."

"I asked him to play dumb, if anyone asks him. He likes you a lot—he won't say anything."

"Great—now he thinks I'm a crook," Steve said, dodging around a bush.

"You can explain it to him however you want, but not until this is all over."

"So where should I say I was, if I get asked?"

"You went to New Mexico," Slater said. "You bought a train ticket and rented a car, after all, so there's an irrefutable trail. But I wasn't there. So don't go telling anyone that I was, because it's not true."

"I get it, Slater," he said irritably. "I'll keep my mouth shut."

"Stop for a second, and cover your eyes. I want to make sure we're headed the right direction." Wincing at the light of his phone's screen, he checked the map and doused it again, then put his hands on Steve's shoulders, adjusting his trajectory. "That way."

After a few more minutes of trudging, Steve said, "I see your car."

When they got back to the vehicle, Slater opened the trunk and stowed the shovel and his gloves, then climbed in the driver's seat. Both of them squinted in the suddenly brilliant dome light.

"Mission accomplished," Slater said, starting the engine and pulling back onto the asphalt.

"Plausible deniability?" Steve said.

"For all of us."

Slater accelerated on the empty road, his headlights illuminating the sparse roadside yuccas and pinyons, casting them in harsh relief against the inky blackness.

"We're not going back to the 40?" Steve asked.

"We're closer to the 15 here."

"So was that really easier than just turning it over to your company?"

"It gives me breathing room to wrap up the case. If I held onto it, the timeline becomes problematic. 'When did you get it' isn't an issue anymore, because I don't have it. Plus I'm not driving around with felony-level stolen goods sitting in my trunk. I can say I got the location as a tip whenever it suits me."

"I get it," Steve said. "As long as no one spills that you're the one who buried it."

"If you say anything about that," Slater said sharply, "I'll plant you out here too."

"Jesus, you're a hard-ass. I was joking. You know me better than that."

"I do know you. Trust, however, is a whole other thing."

Steve scoffed and cranked the back of his seat down, curling up under his jacket.

TWELVE

Slater drove fast on the back road, with no other traffic, eventually merging onto the freeway. He hated the 15, with all the yahoo drivers in the dusty high desert, and even early Sunday morning provided no respite from the traffic.

Pink twilight was breaking when he dropped down into the metropolis and finally got off the freeways onto surface streets. Steve was still fast asleep when he pulled up at the curb in front of his house.

"You're home," Slater said, putting a hand on his shoulder.

Waking up, Steve looked around, caught Slater's eye, and smiled, his eyes sleepy. Such a beautiful man.

"Thanks for driving," Steve said, putting the seat up. "What do we do now?"

"You live your life. Tell people you needed to get away for a few days. You never saw me, and you know nothing about the necklace. If Lillian asks, you don't know where it is."

"She won't buy that."

"You can't wimp out and tell her," Slater said, raising his voice. "That'll put you behind bars along with her, and probably me. Deal with her however you need to, but keep your damn mouth shut."

"OK," he said, frowning.

"You can't get angry at her and decide to report her to the cops either—that ship has sailed. You'll take us all down."

"I understand that."

"I'm putting a lot of trust in you here, Steve. Am I making a mistake?"

"I can do this," he said.

"When's the last time you saw the necklace?"

"Uh …"

"You shouldn't have to think about it. Answer me," Slater demanded.

"The night we went to the opera. At the factory."

"Correct."

"Is someone going to ask me that?"

Slater sighed. "Lillian will."

———·———

The drive home was quick, so early in the day, and it was a relief to watch the garage door roll down behind the Thunderbird. He wanted nothing more than to crash in his own bed, but one last task couldn't wait.

Pulling out his laptop, he spent a few minutes printing out the latitude-longitude screen shot from the desert, as well as the photos he'd taken of the burial site. They were black-and-white renderings, because that's what his printer could do, but the shovel handle and surrounding flora were in sharp focus. Whoever went to dig it up would have clear reference points.

Stapling them together, on the top sheet he scrawled "Location where Kawada necklace is buried, Mojave National Preserve," then put them with the case file from Cudahy Mutual. It would be a shame if that beautiful object were lost forever. This way, Della would get those pages if he died before winding things up. It wasn't the kind of case where Slater was under that kind of threat, but in his line of work he thought about the possibility a lot.

Folding his satchel closed, he took a long pull of bourbon. It seemed decadent to do that at this hour of the morning, but it fit his booze rules— he was going to bed.

In the bedroom he stripped off his clothes and stretched out, grateful to be horizontal, his head sinking into the pillow. At one point he started awake, thinking that he'd drifted into sleep behind the wheel at high speed on a dark highway. Finally, though, he sank into the depths.

It was afternoon when he woke, and as he swam up to full speed, he ran through the last two days in his mind. There was really just one question left, and if things went right, it wouldn't take long to resolve it.

Once he'd microwaved a mug of water to make coffee, he sat in his recliner and went through his messages. Max had texted a couple of hours ago:

She just went out.

He dialed Max's number.

"You're back?" Max asked when he picked up.

"This morning. So Silvana Lee is gone?"

"Actually she's back in her apartment, a couple of minutes ago. I was going to text you."

"Was she alone?"

"The guy wasn't with her. The camera only pinged once, when she left. You were right—she doesn't use her kitchen. She's back now, and I'm sure she's alone."

"Good to know," Slater said.

"If you're going over there, do you need backup?"

"I'll call if I do."

"Or just wave at the kitchen socket."

Once he'd pulled on some clothes, he took his satchel down to the car and locked it in the trunk. On the way downtown he stopped briefly at a supermarket, to buy a single item: the most expensive vegan chocolate bar he could find. It was in a gold-embossed black wrapper and labeled 81% CACAO.

Silvana's neighborhood was quiet, he thought, parking a block away, but then it was probably always this dead, except when the stupid stadium was in use. He didn't bother putting on his ball cap or latex gloves, and made his way to the service bay of the Ampulosa Residences. The master key to the fire stairs was still in his pocket, and he used it to get in, then trotted down a flight, walking through the strange storage-unit parking lot, and up to the fifteenth floor.

Banging on Silvana's door with the heel of his fist elicited no response, but he saw the peephole go dark.

"Let me in," he said, "or I'm coming back with the cops."

Listening, there was no reply, so Slater banged harder. "I know you're in there, Silvana."

Finally a muffled woman's voice said, "Give me a minute."

The peephole brightened again as she stepped away from the door. Slater listened, but there was no sound within. There was no back way out, he knew that. The balcony? He hadn't looked at it very closely, but maybe there was a way to climb into the next apartment.

But the peephole darkened again as she approached, and the door swung open. His first glimpse of her was the back of her head, familiar from the security video at Kawada Couture but in full color now—a riot of streaky blond hair spilling past her shoulders, bouncing as she stepped back into the room. It looked luxurious and expensive, but Brian was right, it had to be a wig.

She went several steps in before she turned to him and folded her arms. Despite being barefoot and dressed in a fluffy white bathrobe, she was in full makeup, and had weirdly luminous blue eyes. He could understand how that had unnerved Carolina.

She didn't seem afraid of him, even though she'd put distance between them. "What do you want?" she demanded.

"To talk," Slater said casually, reaching for the door handle and closing it behind him. "How much did you get from Kawada Couture? Steve wouldn't tell me. It must have been a lot. That was a clever grift."

"Clever of you too, to have found me," she said, raising her eyebrows. "But if you were serious about your moralizing, you would have brought the police with you. I'm thinking that means you want a cut."

Slater knew that voice. It was lower in pitch now, but the enunciation was the same.

"Well, you're out of luck, chump," she continued. "It's all gone."

"Vegas?" Slater asked.

"You've done your homework. It's an expensive place."

"I brought you a gift," he said, stepping toward the sofas that faced each other across a table in front of the balcony doors.

"What's your game?" she demanded, scowling, but watched as he pulled the black-wrapped chocolate out of his pocket and set it on the coffee table. She eyed it, for way too long, and then stepped toward him. "Is this some kind of trick?"

"It's just chocolate," he said. "It's very high in cacao."

"I know," she said, irritated, and dropped onto a sofa, picking it up and studying the wrapper.

Slater sat across from her, arms stretched across the back of the sofa. "Jeff said you had a thing for chocolate. You're really very good—I wasn't completely sure until just now."

Silvana finally looked away from the wrapper and met his gaze. Her eyes were hard, angry, but not fearful. This was no amateur.

"How do you do that thing with your voice?"

Slater asked. "It's much lower than when you're Lillian."

"How did you figure it out?"

"I've known plenty of drag queens over the years. They do the same thing with the makeup, changing the contour of your nose, moving your cheekbones, shaping your eyes. It works really well—unless you get too close. You look like a different person. Enough to fool Carolina, at least."

She looked at the chocolate again, deftly unwrapping one end and taking a bite. Her eyes fluttered closed as she savored it.

"Was it in your pocket?" she said. "It's the perfect temperature. Just slightly softened."

She chewed it with her mouth open, smacking her tongue and breathing in through pursed lips. Slater watched, fascinated. The air flow must heighten the flavors, he decided. Why else would she eat it that way?

The huge wig and the contacts were almost too much, almost like a caricature. But for anyone predisposed to buying it, anyone who felt a stir of attraction for her or saw her flash some cash, it would work, and they'd be dazzled, in the thrall of the glamorous Silvana Lee.

"Is it all for gambling?" Slater asked. "The necklace, and conning Carolina at the factory?"

Silvana opened her eyes and talked through the chocolate. "Jewelry is pretty, but cash is so much more fun. I decided, why not have both?"

"Where did you hide the necklace when the cops came to the factory that night?"

She giggled at the memory. "In my underpants. I knew they'd never frisk me—I was the victim." She took another bite from the bar, enjoying it for a moment with her eyes closed. "You didn't answer my question," she said. "How did you figure it out?"

"Lillian and Silvana both have a taste for Clytemnestra scarves. That's what made Steve suspicious on Thursday."

Silvana scoffed. "Steve is such a boob. He grew up in LA, but he acts like he just fell off the turnip truck."

"He wasn't keeping you in grand enough style? You had to rip him off too?"

"He's a cheap bastard," she said emphatically. "That money is partly mine anyway. Taking it from the factory instead of nagging it out of him means there are no strings attached." She met his gaze. "You said Steve figured it out. Does he actually know Lillian is Silvana?"

"I think it crossed his mind," Slater said. "He said he thought maybe the two were collaborating. An honest man doesn't easily see the intricacies of deceit. Not me, though. I'm used to digging through the trash."

She leaned toward him across the table,

letting her robe fall open. "Please don't tell him," she said, her eyes pleading. "He'll kill me. I just know he will."

Slater glanced at her breasts, perfectly shaped and spilling out of her robe. They must have cost a fortune. "Nice try."

Sitting back, her eyes went dead. "It was worth a shot." She pulled her robe closed. "I thought you were probably gay. I could smell Jeff's stink on you."

"You are going to tell Steve," he said firmly. "Or I will."

Silvana sighed, and closed her eyes, her mouth working the chocolate. "I have a good thing going here. I could totally cut you in. I lied when I said all the money was gone. Plus there's the necklace payout. You can help secure that, and then get some of it for yourself."

"You have to tell him." Slater pulled out his phone and dialed Steve, watching Silvana eat.

Steve picked up and said cheerfully, "Can't get enough of me?"

"I need you to come to the Ampulosa Residences. It's at apartment building in South Park. Unit 1560."

"Why?"

"Just do it," Slater snapped. "It's important."

"My car is still at Union Station."

"Take a ride-share. And come now."

Silvana sneered at him as he ended the call.

"Buzzkill," she said. "You're not the only one with a boyfriend."

"Who is he?"

"Maybe you'll meet him. He should be here any minute."

"You don't seem worried about that," Slater said.

"I still don't see how my scarves could have led you to this building. I've been very careful creating Silvana. She's even got a passport." She looked wistful. "I do love those scarves."

"Why do you have this apartment?" he asked. "It's barely lived in. What else does Silvana do besides the grift?"

"Well, putting on all this makeup takes time. I can't very well entertain my boyfriend at Steve's house either."

The phone on the kitchen counter rang, in two short bursts. Silvana smirked at Slater and rose, picking up the receiver.

She listened, then said, "Send him up."

"The boyfriend?" Slater asked, rising from the sofa.

"You'll love him," she said. "Just your type."

Slater moved toward the door, watching her standing there with her arms folded.

The doorknob rattled, and then came a knock. Silvana frowned. She hadn't expected that, hadn't seen Slater set the deadbolt. She quickly stepped to the door and unlocked it.

The guy filled the door frame, muscular and with oily black hair, wearing a shiny suit like the one in Silvana's closet. This is the guy who wore the ski-size Italian shoes. Most concerning was the bulge under his left arm. Slater had to think fast.

"Hey, baby, you've still got your face on," the guy said, but she stepped back, and his eyes narrowed when he caught sight of Slater.

"Who's this?" he said.

Before she could speak, Slater stepped toward him, flashing his best shit-eating smile and extending his hand. "Slater Ibáñez."

The guy reflexively reached for his hand. "Claudio—"

Slater yanked his hand down and struck his jaw with his left fist. He had to use a lot of force, as this guy was big. Claudio's head spun, but not enough to lose his balance. There was enough time, however, for Slater to reach inside his jacket and yank his weapon out of his holster.

Stepping back toward the kitchen, he leveled it at Claudio, who stepped toward him, rage in his eyes, but then stopped when he saw the muzzle.

"You little fuck," Claudio hissed, but he didn't advance.

"Close the door, Silvana," Slater said, and

when she had, added, "Let's sit down."

Claudio moved slowly toward the sofas, eyeing Slater, who could see the wheels turning.

"Don't even think about it," Slater said, and deftly pulled back on the pistol's slide, audibly racking a round.

Claudio sat on one of the sofas, casually folding one knee over the other, his huge shoe dangling high over the coffee table. Silvana moved to sit beside him, but Slater waved the weapon.

"Other side, sister."

She sat across from Claudio, watching Slater, naked hatred in her eyes.

"You thought Claudio would take care of me, is that it?" Slater demanded. "Maybe rub me out?"

Ignoring him, Silvana reached for the chocolate on the coffee table and took a bite.

"You're from Vegas, I'm thinking," Slater said to Claudio. "Just based on the suit."

His anger at being disarmed seemed to be fading. "I get around," he said, cocking his head.

"I'd say you're definitely a casino goon," Slater said. "Do they pay you very well? I know Silvana is a high-roller. It's such a predictable match—two casino rats. Would you have capped me for her? You wouldn't do that if she was just a customer, but it seems she thought you would. So the question is, is it love, or just a business arrangement?"

Claudio grinned and looked at Silvana, who

was still noisily eating chocolate, then looked back to Slater. "So what are you—South American, or South Asian? Some kind of mutt?"

"I'm the guy with the heater."

"So far, you haven't really pissed me off, *cholo*. Not yet. That means there's still time for you to get out of this situation."

Slater scoffed and waved the weapon. "Let me stop you right there. Don't pretend you're the one in control."

Claudio pressed his lips into a hard line and looked away.

"It's an interesting choice of words," Slater continued, "calling me a *cholo*, which I'm certain has been thrown at you more than once. We need to stick together, brother, not tear each other down."

"You're not my brother," Claudio said.

"Wrong. I'm you, just working for different people. But I will add," he said calmly, "if you insult me one more time, I'll shoot you in the head."

Claudio's eyebrows shot up.

"A shrink once told me that I'm too sensitive," Slater continued, "but I really don't think that's what it is, you know? I think I just don't like to be insulted. Shrinks are fun, but I don't really get the point. They've always told me I need to relax. That's literally the last thing I need," he said emphatically. "It'll be easy to claim self-defense, by the way, because you're the one who brought the weapon." Slater waggled it at him, and looked at Silvana. "It'll be harder to explain why I had to ventilate Lillian here, although I'm sure I'll think of something."

Silvana's mouth was still working the chocolate, a dab of it on her upper lip now. For the first time, she looked unsure.

The house phone rang with the double burst. Slater stepped sideways toward it, not taking his eyes or the weapon off Claudio.

"Steve Kawada is here," the concierge said when he picked up the receiver.

"Send him up," Slater said, and hung up.

"Who's here?" Claudio asked, affecting casual disinterest.

"Her husband," Slater said. "Have you two met?"

Claudio frowned. "You never told me you were married."

"It's not like that, baby," she said, leaning toward him.

"There's no gray area. You're either married or you're not," he said.

Silvana shrugged helplessly.

"What the fuck?" Claudio demanded, his voice rising.

"Shut up, both of you," Slater said sharply, and moved toward the door.

A moment later there was a gentle knock, and Slater called, "It's open." It was indeed Steve, he saw, glancing at him as he entered.

Steve stopped short. "What's with the gun, Slater? You said you didn't have one of those."

"Come in and shut the door," Slater said, not looking at him.

Steve pushed the door closed and stood near it.

"This is Claudio," Slater said, gesturing with the weapon, "and you already know his girlfriend, Silvana Lee."

"Silvana Lee?" Steve said, his voice rising. "How did you find her?"

"I think you already know that. Look closer."

Steve took a few steps toward her, his eyes wide. "Lillian?"

"Hello, darling," she said, waving the wrapper with the half-eaten chocolate.

"It was you," Steve managed, staring at her.

"Sharp as a scalpel, isn't he?" she said, turning to Claudio. "This is what an Ivy League education gets you."

"You look like a drag queen," Steve said.

Slater stifled a laugh, and Silvana said, "Close your mouth, sweetheart. You're gaping."

"You stole from me?" Steve demanded. "Why didn't you just ask me for money?"

"I did," she snapped. "Repeatedly. You held out on me. I had to teach you a lesson."

Steve took a deep breath. "Is he really your boyfriend?"

"In a way," she said, and looked at Claudio. "More like a means to an end. Like a dildo with a casino comp card on the other end."

"You trash bag," Claudio said, glaring at her, his lip curling in a sneer.

"Look in the mirror sometime," she said flatly. "You'll see what trash really looks like."

His face hot, Claudio looked to Slater, who shrugged.

Silvana turned to Steve, smiling sweetly. "He's just an ape, darling. It doesn't change anything between us. We'll get through this. We have before."

Steve just stared at her, his chest heaving.

"Say something," she pleaded, and jutting her chin at Slater, added, "and call off your pit bull."

"Here's what's going to happen," Steve said, his voice low, trembling at first. "You're not coming into my house again. Keep the 'Stang, but that, plus what you stole from the company, is all you get. I'm going to get my lawyer to draw up a divorce settlement, and if you don't sign it on the spot, I'll inform the police about the necklace, and that you dressed up in drag to defraud my company. That would put you behind bars for four to six years, wouldn't you say, Slater?"

"Well," Slater said, affecting thoughtfulness,

"with fraud, double sentencing kicks in once you're over a hundred grand. So you might be looking at more like fifteen to twenty."

Silvana's eyes darted from him to Steve. "It doesn't have to be this way, pumpkin. Let's go to dinner and talk things through."

"No more talking," Steve said, and looking to Slater, "Are you coming? You can drive me to a locksmith. I need to change the locks on my house."

"Is this thing registered?" Slater asked, waggling the weapon at Claudio.

"Not to me," he said.

"Good. What did you pay for it?"

Claudio frowned. "I think it was about three."

"It's nothing personal, but obviously I can't give it back to you. I'm going to leave you three C notes over here."

Stepping into the kitchen, Slater pulled out his wad of cash and peeled off three hundreds, dropping them on the counter, still watching Claudio and Silvana. Reaching behind the sink, he pried his stealth camera out of the socket and pocketed it. It would be impossible to trace to him, but these things were expensive.

With the weapon still trained on Claudio, he moved toward the door, where Steve was waiting.

Rising from the sofa, Silvana held her arms out toward Steve. Her eyes were filled with tears, dark ribbons of mascara running down her cheeks.

"Sit down," Slater barked, training the gun on her.

She fell to her knees instead. "Darling, wait. Please," she sobbed.

"Damn, you're good at this," Slater said. "I almost believe it."

Steve was watching her, his face contorted with emotion. Slater pulled open the door and pulled him out.

"Keep on walking," Slater said, hustling to the elevator. "You know those are crocodile tears."

Once the elevator door closed, Slater took a deep breath to dispel the adrenaline and flipped the safety on the weapon, sliding it into his pants, under the front of his belt.

"What is wrong with me?" Steve demanded.

"Well, you married her."

"Why didn't I see it sooner?"

Slater chuckled, and Steve glared at him.

"You find amusement in my misery?"

"I'm just happy that's what you're thinking. If you were all sad and heartbroken, I'd be worried."

Steve watched him for a moment. "I guess that'll come later."

"As long as you don't change your mind about everything you just said to her."

"No way."

The elevator doors rumbled open, and Slater stepped off.

"You overshot the lobby. This is the parking garage," Steve said.

"We're going out the back way." Slater led him to the fire stairs, then out to the side street and the Thunderbird.

"Why did I marry her?" Steve said, climbing into the passenger's seat.

Slater started the car and shrugged. "The cock wants what the cock wants."

Steve turned to stare at him. "Such a romantic."

———◆———

When he dropped Steve at his house, he spent a minute texting him the number of a locksmith that Slater worked with who wouldn't rip him off for coming out on a Sunday.

Steve climbed out, and before closing the door, stooped to look back in at Slater and meet his eye. "Thanks for telling me."

"The truth isn't always pretty, but it's usually the best option."

Steve nodded, but he looked lost.

"You're going to be fine."

"I know," he said quietly, and stepped back, closing the door.

As he pulled away, Slater saw him in the rearview, standing there watching him leave.

It was a relief to be done with this, to have everything almost settled. There was a report to write for Della, with the location of the necklace. She wouldn't ask any questions about how it got there, as long as Cudahy Mutual got it back. Stopped at a red light, he spotted a magnolia up the block, finally leafing out around the blossoms. Spring was close.

Walking from the parking lot across to his office, he could feel Claudio's weapon, way too close to his junk. Max would know what to do with it, how to bust it up and ditch the pieces in the trash. Stepping off the elevator, fishing for his keys, he broke into a broad smile when he saw the office door:

SLATER IBÁÑEZ
MAXIMILLIAN CONROY
INVESTIGATIONS

Max had given him top billing. He didn't have to do that, but it certainly felt good.

Also from Dagmar Miura

That First Heady Burn

The first book in the Slater Ibáñez series sees Slater running surveillance on an injured tech worker and tangling with blackmailers, party girls, late-night hookups with a gamut of guys, and a lot of bourbon.

slater.dagmarmiura.com

The Mason Braithwaite Paranormal Mystery Series

No one is ever quite sure whether psychic investigator Mason gets results with actual psychic power or his more mundane flatfooting, but the disheveled redhead manages to resolve some intractable mysteries.

mason.dagmarmiura.com

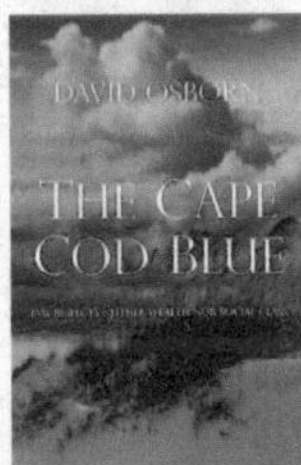

The Cape Cod Blue

The glittering, exalted world of art auctioning hides love, hate, and parricidal murder in a wealthy and socially prominent family when forgery of an anonymous Cape Cod painting is used to steal a world-famous portrait that's worth a fortune.

capecod.dagmarmiura.com

The Bone Bridge

Yarrott Benz, the 2016 Ippy Award winner for memoir, is forced to deal with extraordinary self-sacrifice in this harrowing account of teenage brothers, as different as night and day, trapped together in a dramatic medical dilemma.

bonebridge.dagmarmiura.com

www.ingramcontent.com/pod-product-compliance
Lightning Source LLC
Chambersburg PA
CBHW010348170726
48284CB00011B/2837